The Souvenir
PATRICIA CARLON

The Souvenir

PATRICIA CARLON

SOHO

This edition published by arrangement with Wakefield Press, Australia

First published in Great Britain by Hodder and Stoughton, 1970; first published in the United States of America in 1996

Published by
Soho Press, Inc.
853 Broadway
New York, N.Y. 10003

Library of Congress Cataloging-in-Publication Data

Carlon Patricia, 1927—
The souvenir / Patricia Carlon.
p.   cm.
ISBN 1-56947-065-0 (alk. paper)
1. Private investigators—Australia—Fiction.   I. Title.
PR9619.3.C37S58   1996
823—dc20
95-18477
CIP

Manufactured in the United States of America
10 9 8 7 6 5 4 3 2 1

The Souvenir
PATRICIA CARLON

Marion walked through the door with the plain black letter-
ing saying, 'Jefferson Shields', to disappointment, and one so
great that she was sure the whole strength of it showed on her
face.

Embarrassment held her rigid just inside the door, till he
stood up and came round behind her, shutting the door, ges-
turing her to the black leather chair by the desk.

She moved jerkily, the briefcase banging across her slim
legs. Immediately she sank into the leather chair. She reached
for a cigarette, then was sorry because her hand was noticeably shaking and he must have seen the fact when he reached
towards her with the lighter.

He went back to sit down then, still not having spoken to
her, a small, thin man who was a study in grey – grey hair,
grey rimmed spectacles, neat grey suiting. A nonentity of a
man who might have been a clerk in some undistinguished
office. One could imagine him worrying over his mortgage or
his garden or his children. Marion couldn't imagine him
doing the impossible, and the disappointment came sweeping
back.

She said abruptly, 'I was told you solve puzzles.'

He made no attempt to help her go on and that made her
angry. Her nervousness went. She leaned forwards in the
chair to toss at him, 'I've a puzzle that's baffled everyone for
four years.'

'By everyone, you mean?' The tone was as dry and colourless and lacking in force as the man.

'The police. The press. Dozens of ordinary people, including myself.' She added again, 'I was told you solve puzzles.'

Her gaze skimmed over the room. She was disappointed in that, too. It could have been any business office of the better type – grey carpet, good leather chairs, a shiny desk, a bookcase – there was nothing to distinguish it from a hundred others.

He asked, 'What did you expect to see?' A faint tinge of irony entered the voice. 'You looked quite disapproving when you gazed around. What did you expect to see?'

She shook her head. Half in exasperation, half in self-amusement, she admitted, 'I don't know. Anything, I suppose, except an ordinary office.'

'Perhaps a little magic?' He shook his head, spread his hands wide in dismissal. 'I don't deal in magic. If you've come to ask that I perform some species of magic – a miracle – you're wasting your time.'

Marion looked down at the briefcase on her knee. She said, 'You performed a miracle once. I read about it. You found a woman. She had been missing for a long, long time. You found . . .'

'That wasn't a miracle. I was given facts and I studied them till I saw something no one else had. I'll give you an example. Look into a mirror at your features. Study them as closely as you can. An hour later go back and do it again and again later. Keep going back. Before you come to the end of the exercise you'll have discovered a new face. I don't deal in magic. I deal in facts.'

She looked down at the briefcase.

'And puzzles,' she reminded him sharply. She touched the briefcase. 'I've all the facts you can find, and the rumours, and the press reports and statements and interviews. I know the facts. I want an answer to them.'

She lifted her head. 'Do the names Peta Squire and Sandra Kilby mean anything to you?'

She waited patiently till he shook his head. 'Most people have forgotten,' she admitted. 'It's four years ago. Four years this January, when they were sixteen years old. One of them killed a man. One of them stabbed at him, once, twice, brutally, in a blind rage, and killed him. His name was Jack Burton.' She saw the quick lift of his head. 'You're remembering now, aren't you? Did you ever wonder what happened in the end? Nothing did. One of them killed him and each accused the other. One told a story that was lies. She lied so well no one has ever found out which of them lied.

'So, nothing happened.'

The air-conditioned chill of the office seemed to strike through her whole body. She wished that there was something to draw over the bare-armed sheath of striped silk. Her white gloved hands tightened over the briefcase in an effort to still her body against her shivering.

She told him, 'I've spoken to the man who was in charge of all the enquiry. His name is Podmore. Inspector Podmore. I reminded him that nothing had ever happened.' Her forehead, under the black fringe, was corrugated in ugly lines, as she tried to remember that dingy office and the voice of the other man. 'He asked me what I imagined a jury did. He wanted to know if I imagined that in a jury room they tossed a coin, heads for one verdict, tails for the other. He told me it would have had to come to that, or a complete farce. He said that in any case it could never even have come to a trial, because the word of one weighed no heavier than the word of the other.

'He said, "If I had caught one out in just one lie! There wasn't so much as one I could find. I couldn't touch either of them." He told me that if he could have credited such cunning and the ability to carry it off, he might have believed they'd done it together for some unknown reason and fashioned two stories, so perfect, so unbreakable, so closely dovetailing, that it was a foregone conclusion that neither of them could ever be touched by the law.'

She shook her dark head almost violently. 'He didn't believe that though. They were sixteen years old.' Her soft voice broke on the words, then strengthened. 'He couldn't give belief, either, to the idea that the one who lied thought up all that story by herself, and had the strength to stick to it, without help. He told me that one set of parents had had to lie, too. There'd been time, he reminded me, for the story to be rounded and perfected and polished before the world ever heard it.'

She leaned forward again. 'I have to know which one lied.'

'Why? Your name is Burton. There was a sister – '

She brushed that aside with the impatient admission, 'Yes, I'm Jack's sister.'

The grey eyes appraised her. 'You were barely older than the girls yourself.'

'I was nineteen. I'm twenty-three now.'

'And those two girls are women of twenty. A woman of twenty has more reasons than a child of sixteen for hiding an unpleasant truth. Have you considered that point? Four years ago they were children. In the eyes of the law at any rate. Almost certainly, if one had been sent to a corrective home, she would have been released by now. Try to imagine the difference if she is found out today, next week, next month. She will have to stand trial, as a woman, not a child, and as a woman she will have to admit that for four years she has left another woman under a shadow of guilt. Four years ago, if she had been found out the crime would have been seen as the result of a child's panic.'

His voice was demanding. 'Four years ago you were nineteen. Jack Burton was your brother. You had a valid reason, and were grown-up enough to demand the enquiry be kept open. Why didn't you?'

'Actually I don't know, or rather I was sick of it, you see. People can be terrible.' The long shiver couldn't be controlled no matter how tightly her gloved hands fastened on the briefcase. 'Even when they're sorry for you they can be terrible.

You're news. They look at you, and you know they're noting everything about you and that later on every emotion you show is going to be public property, a conversation piece for the dinner table.'

A faint smile touched the stiffness of her mouth. 'I sound bitter, don't I? I'm not really. Not now. You grow older and you see things in another perspective and you realise that for other people it was all a nine-day wonder that they'd be hard put to remember now.'

She shook her head quickly, 'But that's hardly an answer, except I was just glad that it all died down and I could crawl into a corner somewhere without someone reminding poor Marion of her loss and pulling me out of my corner. Nothing anyone did was going to bring Jack back home. I know it must sound odd' – her voice was faintly apologetic – 'but I couldn't even feel vindictive. I was angry, I suppose, and bitter.' She shook her head. 'Well, anyway, there seemed nothing more to do.'

'Yet four years later you've come to me. What's happened now that makes you think something can be done?'

She had to admit, 'Nothing. Nothing at all. I just want to find out the truth of it.'

'You said you *had* to find out which one lied,' he reminded her.

She was angry again. She said rapidly, 'I want to get married. At least – there's someone I'd like to marry. If he asked me. I doubt if he will. You see, he's Peta Squire's stepbrother. Oh, no relation – no blood-relation, I mean – at all. He's older than Peta. He went away when his father married Peta's mother. He hardly knew Peta at all.

'It's odd, ridiculous, how things turn out, isn't it? I'd never met any of them you know. They didn't even appear at the inquest. There were a whole line of doctors to say Sandra Kilby was ill. I suppose everyone would have thought it looked bad if Peta had been made to appear. So she didn't either. There were just statements – read out in court. They're in here.' She tapped the briefcase.

'There wasn't so much as a photo of the girls in any paper. I think that's the law, isn't it? When it's a case of juveniles?' At his nod she went on, 'And there was just a blurred one of Peta's people. There were lots of Jack, though. Me too.

'I thought I'd altered a lot, but Ward recognised me. It was a party, and I looked round, and he was staring at me. He looked terribly upset. I wondered why, and then someone noticed us staring at each other and jumped in to introduce us. I thought he was going to run away. He didn't though.'

She shook her head. 'But that isn't part of this,' she tapped the briefcase. 'Except – one set of parents lied, you understand. Oh yes, they did it to protect her – the girl who killed Jack, but they lied, and they kept on lying. They've held to those lies for four years, and the one who's innocent, and her family, have suffered for it.'

For a moment she was silent, lost in thought, then she added, 'He said – Inspector Podmore, I mean – he said that one lot of parents had had to know. He said, "Even if they didn't know, right at first, if she told them just a garbled story, the best she could think of, anything at all so long as it cleared her from coming trouble, they'd have probed and questioned and they'd have kept on at it."'

She lifted her gaze to meet the grey spectacled face across the desk. 'He's right you know, when he claimed that some time there had to be a moment when they knew she was lying. You can't live with a child and love it and help it to grow up and fuss over it and scold it and punish it, without there being some way you can tell what's lies, what's truth. Oh, for a little while you might be fooled. He said that, but not for ever. Not for an enquiry that takes months and months and months.

'It did, you see. For nearly six months the police kept going back and questioning. They probed into every aspect of the girls' lives. They questioned their friends again and their teachers – everyone. They came back over and over again and went over those stories uncounted times, and there was never anything, never a moment when the police could say, "You're lying." But one set of parents must have known.

'All those long months the one who lied never broke down, never faltered. He said, "It was incredible. You can lie in desperation, but there comes a point where the whole world seems against you and you can't go it alone any more. You have to tell the truth to someone and unburden yourself, but those girls never faltered, never broke down. If you're innocent you've an armour of sorts, and after all, there's nothing to unburden except what you've already told. But the other one – she had to have another armour – the knowledge that someone else shared the truth; a relief of mind that she'd unburdened herself; a knowledge that her lies would be backed up, for ever. She knew, I'm certain of it, that her parents would go on lying. They knew all right.'

She hesitated again, then told him. 'He – Inspector Podmore – told me that after six months there was a lull. They let the case seemingly slide. Then, after months of inaction, they suddenly returned. They were hoping, you see, they'd catch one girl off guard. Only they didn't. If I marry Ward I want to know where I stand. I want to be able to talk to Ward's family and be part of it.'

'You've made up your mind that it was Sandra Kilby who lied?' he asked condemningly. She realised that and denied the suggestion.

She said angrily, 'You didn't let me finish. I don't know which one lied. Have you ever wondered how something like this affects the *family* concerned? Sandra's parents got a divorce. No, I don't know why, but Sandra lives alone with her mother now. She's a secretary. And Peta has gone away. She's made a world of her own. She moved away as soon as she could – barely a year later. She lives in a tiny flat and she illustrates books.

'Ward went away, too. Right away. You see, he's like me. He couldn't stand not knowing. If I marry him, he's going to go further away still. I'll be an embarrassment to everyone, and I couldn't face them anyway. Can't you see how horrible it's all going to be?' She pleaded at his grey unresponsive feature. 'If I know they lied, I can take Ward away, and I won't care about it, and we'll never see them again. If they didn't – I want Ward to go back.

'There's the girl who's innocent too. I know I sound as if I'm thinking only of myself, but I've thought of her, too. And her family.

'One of them lied. I want you to tell me which one. One of them killed my brother. I want to know which one. It's all here,' she tapped the briefcase again. 'It – everything – all that happened after, began when Peta and Sandra met at Central Station.'

2

SANDRA

The too-pale face gazed back at her, round-eyed, from the smudged mirror surface and the lips mouthed at her softly, 'All right, so you're here.' The small head, with the long single plait of thick fair hair, nodded gravely, almost grimly at her from the glass. 'You wanted it just this way,' she reminded. 'You said, and you said it loud and you said it over and over till you and all of them were just plain sick of the sound of it – "No family, no fussing." So, all *right*, Sandra Kilby, you have it the way you wanted. No family, no fussing, and the sort of holiday you nagged and coaxed to get. So why go on just standing, when the train's out there, waiting? It's going to move soon. Too soon for you if you're not careful, and what're you going to do if you have to go back and walk in the front door and face them and admit that you didn't go after all because you developed butterflies and the wobbles and just couldn't face breaking the ice, and – *mixing*? You can't admit that you felt so alone you had to go back.'

'You do that' – her pale reflection warned her – 'and you'll never get away again. It'll always be a hotel and dressing for dinner, and them saying to keep away from the crowd on the sands, because most of them don't look nice, and the sort we're used to meeting at home.'

It was never any good saying that if you wanted to meet the sort of person you met around home you might as well stay there and not go a hundred miles away, but that if you did go a hundred miles you wanted to meet another sort of person altogether, you were simply told not to be silly. Just as she was going to be told if she didn't catch the train waiting out there for her. She'd go back, and they would all smile little secret smiles, and her mother would say, 'Well, you'll never be silly again, now will you, Sandra?' and she'd have to agree that she wouldn't, because there would be nothing else to say, and afterwards, for every summer, there would be dressing for dinner, and the cold chill of a big hotel and –

'Do you want that, Sandra?' her reflection mouthed.

'No!'

She said it aloud, explosively, the sound ripping through the soured-disinfectant smell of the washroom, bouncing back at her from the sweaty-looking tiles, so that a dozen voices seemed to be echoing her denial. Heads turned, reflected in other mirrors. It seemed to her shamed glance that there were hundreds of heads turning, hundreds of eyes staring in wonder. She bent, reached towards the rucksack, scrabbling her toilet things from the shelf, dropping them into the shelter of the canvas, trying to hide from those curious eyes.

When she looked up again there was only one pair of eyes – deep-set bright blue eyes, regarding her down the sun-burned slide of a too-long nose.

The voice that asked, 'What's the panic?' was unexpectedly deep.

Sandra, still hunched over the rucksack, flicked her gaze up – and up – yet, when she stood, the other girl wasn't so much taller than herself. It was, Sandra realised, the tightness of jeans and checked shirt, clinging to the girl's flesh-pared bones, that had made her for one instant a freakishly towering column of height and no breadth.

The deep voice demanded again, 'What's the panic?' and when Sandra only went on staring, mocked at her.

'You yelled out, "No!" like the village maiden repulsing the lecherous baron, down at the Music Hall. Why? And you needn't bother saying it's none of my business and please go away.' Shrewdly she thrust, 'You were going to say just that, weren't you?'

The thin figure bent, the deep blue gaze taking in the rucksack and the name tape. 'Weren't you S.T. Kilby? I was watching you. I could see you and the little wobbly reflection of you in this mirror here, in that one over there' – a brown thumb jerked backwards – 'and you didn't seem like you cared for your face or anything else. Why not?'

Sandra hefted the rucksack. She demanded, 'Do you go around asking questions all – '

'Yes.' White teeth flashed in a wide smile in the sunburned brown of the thin face. 'Ask a question and break the ice, and believe me, S. Kilby, you look like you've a whole deep freeze to get through.'

She bent, hefting a rucksack almost identical to Sandra's own grey canvas one. 'You've got a pack. So've I. You're alone. So'm I. You didn't want to go out of here – it's written all over you. You'd rather stick the drain perfume – Chanel Central Railway – than go on out there and get into a train.'

The anger of embarrassment stammered Sandra's, 'What a-about yourself? Were you j-just staring at me because *you* didn't want to go out and – '

'No.' The glance down the long sunburned nose was contemptuous. 'I go off every summer. I've done it two years now. I used to go with the church missionaries. My mother was real hot on church missionaries, would you believe? Good works, and rice pudding and a nice swim before breakfast, and pressing flowers and prayers every four hours, like giving milk to babies on schedule. Four-hour feeds of godliness and rice pudding, could you credit I had that? Then I turned fourteen and I said any more rice pudding holidays would give me indigestion, and what about hostelling for a nice change? My mother saw the light – mind you, it took argument, but she saw it, so I've been hostelling two years. It's the first summer for you though, isn't it, S. Kilby?'

Sandra said tautly, 'It's Sandra – my name.'

'I'll call you Sandy,' was the prompt retort.

Sandra said only, 'If you must know, this is the very first summer I've been on my own – '

'Church missionaries and rice pudding?' the deep voice mocked.

'No. A seafront hotel – '

'And family in the background?' The wide smile crossed the sunburned face again. 'I knew it. You looked as if you didn't know what to do next, and anyway, second time round, most everyone has lined up a walk-mate – '

'You said you were alone,' Sandy pointed out.

Equably the other girl answered, 'I said, *most* everyone. You're wiser not to. So all right, you make a friend hostelling one year and you say, "Make a date next summer," and all right, maybe it works. Maybe it doesn't, though. A year's a long time. People change. The one you liked last summer might've altered a whole lot. Got herself a boy maybe and talks of nothing else and talks all day and night. That was what I had last year. It was her boy, or worrying about her complexion because he didn't like freckles and worrying about diet because he didn't like fat and – oh well, it was hell. This year I planned on picking up someone along the way.' Her gaze was shrewd, calculating, running over Sandra in appraisal. 'There's no obligation either side that way. You make plans before you go, you're stuck with the one you started out with. Pick up a hitch-mate on the route and if you don't mix well it's goodbye and no harm done.'

Sandra's fair head was lowered, her finger picking at the buckle on the grey canvas. 'You're going to hitch-hike?'

The long thin arms were thrown wide. 'For love's sake, do I look like I run to coach fares?' The dark blue eyes narrowed. 'Why? You're planning on taking coaches?'

'I hadn't planned anything.'

'Except getting away from the family and the seafront hotel – oh, I can guess. Maybe' – the deep voice poked shrewdly – 'your old folks said, "Nice girls don't hitch-hike, Sandra Kilby"? Well?'

'Perhaps they did, perhaps they didn't.' It was time for some show of spirit at least, Sandra decided. She was tired of answering questions, of being summed up and appraised by those deep-set eyes. She hefted the rucksack again, 'I've got a train to catch.' She wasn't going to answer which one, she decided. She wasn't sure she wanted company now. The ice – the deep freeze as the other girl called it – around her head had broken. She felt a rising self-confidence, an eagerness now to get out to the train and look at faces and people and perhaps strike up talk with some of them.

She knew dismay when the deep voice said, 'That'll be the nine-six.' The voice mocked again. 'You think maybe you're the only one with the idea of taking the first train west today? If you go out to platform five now you'll trip over dozens of packs just like yours, Sandy Kilby, and you'd better go out right now or you're going to spend the trip sitting on that same rucksack on the floor.'

Tartly, Sandra thrust back, '*You* don't seem to be worrying about that.'

The white grin creased the sunburned face again. 'You meet good friends on the floor. You ever tried being stand-offish with someone whose knee's touching yours?' She swung her own pack, moving with long swinging strides for the glass doors. Hand outstretched to them, she looked back. Her voice mocked Sandra's indecision, her holding back. 'Scared?' Then half in impatience she added, 'I'll see you safely on the train anyway. Come along, for love's sake. You'll get lost or strayed otherwise, and I'll have you on my conscience. If you don't want to walk with me after, all right. So you needn't. Oh, your face gave you away when I gave you the chance of suggesting it. You didn't, and your face closed up tight. So, all right.'

Sandra burst into an embarrassed babble of speech. 'It wasn't that I didn't want to, it was I was scared I guess, and I hadn't really planned on hitch-hiking, and you're going to, and well – '

The thin shoulders in the checked shirt lifted and shrugged. 'Come along, for love's sake, or both of us'll miss the train.' Her brown hand reached out, catching at Sandra's arm, dragging her through the doorway and out.

Sound hit at them – a long gusty breath of it borne on hot, dusty breeze. The thin figure at Sandy's side ejaculated a long-drawn, 'P-phew! We're going to cook this summer. You're a bit of a nut starting off walking with a skin like that. Whyn't you brown up a bit on the beaches at weekends?'

'Study. I had to study.'

'For love's sake, couldn't you take your books to the beach? You're going to burn now. Serve you right for not using your brains for more than study. You going to worry over your boyfriend at home not liking you maybe if you turn up with freckles?'

Sandra couldn't answer. She was being dragged through the crowds, banging against bodies and cases and oddly shaped packages, trying to apologise, the words lost as she was parted again from the person she'd brushed against. Her ticket was taken from her by the slim brown fingers, thrust at the porter, received back and thrust into the pocket of the checked shirt.

Sandra gasped, 'My ticket – '

'It's all right, I have it. Concentrate on getting through that crowd. Haven't you any elbows to use? There – in there and *shove*!'

The thin brown face was alight with laughter as the pair of them subsided into the comfort of leather seats. 'There,' the deep voice was triumphant, 'would you've got a seat by your own?'

'No,' Sandra admitted. Her gaze was on the faded name-tag on the rucksack the other was holding. Abruptly a slim brown hand covered it, then slowly dropped away again.

The deep voice stated flatly, 'Wincham – that's not my name. My mother's hot on me using it, that's all. Legally it's Squire. Peta Squire. My father was Peter Squire. I can't see any reason, can you, for me using my step-father's name, not even if they'd – him and my mother or is it he and my mother? My teacher's always on to me about slipping up like that – all right, I'll say rather, my step-dad and my mother are real keen on me being a Wincham. I can't see any reason at all for it!' The voice was almost violent in the denial. Then looking into Sandra's withdrawn expression she laughed again, 'So, all right, it's not nice to let your pants or your temper show. That's what my mother says. A lady doesn't show her pants or her temper, and he's not so bad really, but dull.

'Look,' her hand touched Sandra's arm, holding it tightly against withdrawal, 'Have you anything against the idea of hitch-hiking?'

'No.' Sandra looked down at her linked hands in the lap of her blue jeans. 'It's just, well' – a sudden smile touched her mouth – 'how the family looks at it is the way your mother looks at temper, I guess. It's just something a lady doesn't do. Maybe I can't put myself in the picture either – I mean, I just can't imagine standing by the road and having the nerve to ask someone to carry me along on a free passage – '

'I'll tell you something.' Peta had linked her hands now behind her brown head. 'One time my first summer I hitched with a woman. You know what – she was so lonely she went looking for hitch-hikers to talk to her. No, I'm not making it up. Oh, I expect she was a bit nuts. She told us – I'd chummed up with someone by then – she'd nursed an old aunt and the old lady'd been beyond speech and there were no visitors except the doctor and she told us she reckoned how she'd just lost the knack of talking and she'd tried joining clubs only they expected her to do her share of conversation and she had nothing to say, but young people hitch-hiking always had plenty to say and made her feel part of the world again.

'Oh, yes, I reckon she was half nuts, but the point I'm making is that a lot of times you earn your passage. It's not free. Like, sometimes the car's not so hot. You're insurance in case a good hard push uphill's needed. Then, if someone's taking a real long drive, they feel sleepy and if they've someone to talk to they don't drop of at the wheel.

'Anyway' – the linked hands parted and spread out in a little gesture of finality – 'everyone does it.'

With the deep voice silent at her side, Sandra was suddenly conscious of the roar of noise surrounding them. The train had started moving, and she hadn't been aware of that either, and the carriage was packed, the long corridor jammed with a jumble of youthful figures, battered packs and parcels, and even, to her open-eyed surprise, a canary in a blue cage, perched on one rucksack.

She and Peta, part of the crowd, were isolated in a tiny patch of stillness in the whirlpool of talk, screech and wail of transistors, and rumble of train wheels. The canary's tiny beak was opening and shutting, too, but his contribution to the babble was lost. Sandra's fascinated gaze was fastened on the bird. She asked, 'Did you see there's a canary?'

Peta leaned forward, hunching up her jean-clad knees and linking her arms round them. 'I wish I'd thought of that.' Her gaze was reflective when Sandra turned to her, and half impatiently Peta explained, 'You have to have a gimmick. In summer anyway, when all the students are hitch-hiking. There's too much competition. Don't get it, do you?' Her eyes mocked. 'Well, look, if you were driving and saw a couple with a canary in a cage, wouldn't you be more likely to pull up? Canaries are deadly respectable, S. Kilby. They go with tea cosies and crumpets and hand-crocheted tablecloths, and they're good conversation starters. Like having your jacket with a big picture of Switzerland or a map of France on it. They think then you're a foreigner and interesting or odd. Haven't you noticed how people expect foreigners to be one or the other – never normal like folks at home?

'You need a gimmick. There was one chap last summer always wore a top hat. It looked real mad, but it pulled the cars up. They couldn't resist asking about it.'

The deep voice probed, 'Have you a gimmick, S. Kilby? But then, you wouldn't have. You'd planned on going around by coach and bus, hadn't you? Pity it's none of the students, no one young's going to be with you. You're going to be stuck with the middle-agers, the ones with spare cash and creaky bones.'

Because she didn't want to admit that that was her own fear – that the whole trip was going to prove deadly dull, because everyone her own age would be with friends or planning to hitch-hike across country – Sandra thrust the probing aside with a sharp, 'Have you a gimmick yourself? Where's your canary, P. Squire?' Her voice mocked at the other's mockery, 'And your top hat?'

Peta's face creased into open laughter, then sobered. 'I won't tell. Not unless you join up with me. I'm not telling anyone else – they'd try to pinch the idea.'

She stopped, began softly humming under her breath, swaying in time to the music from a nearby transistor, taking up the tune, forming it into words, throwing back her head and letting her deep voice ring out. In a minute the carriage was filled with singing, with laughing faces and swaying bodies.

After a long moment Sandra's wavering treble joined in.

She had known quite well that Peta was watching her, and waiting, but deliberately she had turned her back. She wasn't sure that she wanted to hike through the days ahead with the older girl at her side – talking all the time. That, she decided, standing there, gaze going over the platform, was one reason she was holding back – Peta talked too much, rushed too much. She gave the impression of sweeping along somewhere at some frantic pace, wanting to carry everyone with her, wanting to boss them, too.

It would, Sandra reflected, be a case of them always doing what Peta wanted. Slowly her gaze went over the thinning crowd. It had seemed as though half the whole world had poured out of the train when it had pulled into Moorowie. She had been pushed and jostled, separated from Peta, and had looked hopefully at each passing face, expecting that at any second a hand would touch and hold her arm and someone of the crowd she'd sung and talked to would invite her to come along.

It hadn't happened. Everyone had swept away, still pushing and shoving, leaving herself and Peta and only a few others – lone ones too – standing awkwardly waiting, and waiting, Sandra was sure, like herself, for something expected and hoped for to happen to sweep them along out of the station and away to adventure. As the seconds ticked on, she could see the expectancy and hope slide away from the faces. She wondered if her own face was betraying her to them, meeting the corner-eyed glances thrust her way glances that moved sharply on to another face the minute she met the glance squarely.

I ought to go up to one of them and speak and say out loud, 'Are you alone too?' and break the ice, she told herself and knew that she wasn't going to, because it was obvious that this flotsam of the railway terminus was like herself – altogether new to walking and hitch-hiking and hostelling and all the rest of adventure.

When the deep voice asked at her side, 'Decided what to do yet?' she turned eagerly.

She answered breathlessly, afraid now that Peta would leave her alone in this new world, 'Yes – I'm going to hitch-hike, if I can come along with you. I wouldn't be game on my own.'

Her voice was humble, almost pleading, in that over-whelming eagerness not to be left alone, but if the older girl noticed it she wasn't in the mood for mocking. She said only, 'So all right, but I'm not promising anything. We'll join up for today, tomorrow, too, perhaps and then if we don't find something in it for both of us it'll be goodbye.'

She started for the station exit with a long easy stride, not looking back. Sandra had to grab her pack and run to keep up with her. Only by the exit did she gasp, 'You still have my ticket!' Then at the mocking grin thrust at her over Peta's shoulder she stopped. She started to say, 'You *knew* I'd come –'

'Why'd you think I stayed round, for love's sake? If I'd walked off and left you you'd have been on my conscience, but' – the deep voice held warning – 'like I said, no promises. If it doesn't look like working out, you'll have to chum up with someone else.' The easy stride carried her through the turnstile, outside and left down the road, past shop fronts, with Sandra half skipping behind her.

Outside a delicatessen Peta stopped. She said, 'It had better be ham sandwiches. They're filling and you get proteins. My mother's real hot on proteins. You can buy four and watch they really butter the bread. This' – her white teeth flashed in a quick smile – 'is educating you Sandy Kilby – making you stand up for yourself. You inspect that bread real well. Make them show it to you – remind them you're paying for real butter and want to see it. You needn't look so horrified. You have to learn not to get rooked.

'We'll eat in the Ladies and I'll show you my gimmick, and then we'll try our luck *there*,' she pointed. 'We're going to hitch south first, and don't look so saucer-eyed. You'll get west soon enough, but you go down the west road a bit and you'll see every last one off that train trying to hitch. We'll be all day and get nowhere, so we'll circle round. You get those sandwiches and hurry up.'

It was possible to eat ham and enjoy it in the soured-sweat smell of a petrol station washroom. Sandra discovered that, after the discovery that it was quite possible to demand butter on your bread. She was actually enjoying herself when Peta opened her pack and pulled out a roll of striped silk, spreading it for inspection.

'There you see,' her voice was triumphant, 'it's a clown's rig. I've had it planned right from last summer. It's cool – you feel – and I can get away with just pants and a bra under and it'll cover all my skin from burning and do you reckon anyone could drive past a walking clown without at least pulling up to ask how come?

'I'll change again before we go to the hostels at night and I can wash and dry this out in a few minutes at a laundromat. That's a real good point, because I don't want anyone seeing it and pinching the idea. If you had half a dozen clowns on the move it'd be worse than not having a gimmick at all.'

Sandra sat silent. The thought of actually walking out of the washroom, in company with a clown in full rig, complete with a false red nose, was thoroughly unnerving, but it was just as with everything else in her day since meeting the other girl – she was swept away on Peta's barrage of talk, carried along with the stream of Peta's self-confidence, and borne out again into the blazing afternoon sunshine, and the first hitch was so incredibly easy, so swift, that she echoed Peta's own little triumphant laugh as the pair of them settled into the car's comfort.

Lazily, from the back seat, she listened to Peta's deep voice, mocking, 'A fancy dress party? Oh no, it was this way. You see, our house was burnt down and when my mother went to the Salvation Army the only thing they had for a beanpole like me was this clown's outfit – '

Her explanation to their second driver was hissed, 'Don't let on, but I just escaped from the girls' lockup. Dressed myself up from the stage box, and escaped in a truck load of garbage cans.'

The drivers loved it. They enjoyed every one of the tall tales Peta spun them, and by evening the two girls were dropped in open bushland with only a short stretch to walk to the barrack-like building that housed the hostel.

They stood in a swirl of dust, waving goodbye to the driver, before Peta dragged her companion into the shadows of the ghost gums. In triumph she threw her arm round Sandra's shoulders, hugging her, whispering, 'Wasn't I right? Wasn't I just *right*?' She pulled her further into the shadows, dancing away then, the striped cream silk merging into the streaked trunks of the trees, till Sandra, suddenly frightened of losing her completely from sight, ran after her, calling. Like a mocking will-o'-wisp Peta kept dancing further and further into the tree-deepening shadows. Only when Sandra called her name in real panic did she stop.

'Baby!' the voice mocked among the trees. 'I always have to let off steam when I've been cooped up in a car. I'll change back to jeans and we'll slog up to the hostel. How' – she was pulling shirt and jeans from her pack – 'do you like hitch-hiking now?'

Sandra let her own pack slide to the ground and sank down, crosslegged on top of it. She said, 'Fine' with real enthusiasm, but her mind was on her fear of the ghost gums and the darkness between them.

'With luck we'll be over the mountains tomorrow,' Peta promised her, wriggling into the shirt, slicking back her brown hair with the flat of her hands. 'Come along now, but if they start up there' – she jerked a thumb – 'to talk about gimmicks don't give mine away.'

Gimmicks were hardly touched on. By the time everyone was in the long dormitory, Sandra's head was spinning with tiredness and the babble of talk. With Peta there was never silence, aloneness. From the minute they had walked through the front door of the building they had become part of a crowd talking, laughing, planning. It had been wonderfully exhilarating, but exhausting. There in the long dormitory with the night stars a cluster of brilliance outside the uncurtained open windows, Sandra wanted only sleep, but it refused to come.

She lay quite still, listening. There was the murmur of someone whispering in dreams, a faintly rising snore, the crack and rustle of someone turning over.

She turned her head. There was light enough to see Peta. She was sitting on the bunk, cross-legged, the starlight taking all colour from the blue pyjamas. Taking the sunburn from her face too, so that it looked ghostlike as she turned sharply at Sandra's whisper.

The thin hands closed protectively over what they held, then relaxed, and opened, so that Sandra could see the soft glow of the silver ball, but Peta's deep whisper scorned her own surprised one. Peta denied, 'It's not silver. Chrome. Look at it.' She turned it slowly. 'A perfect little map of the world. My first souvenir of the summer. Didn't you see it for yourself?' The deep voice rose in impatience, then hastily dropped. 'It was the mascot of that little green van. You don't use your eyes, S. Kilby, that's what. World Wide Novelties, it said on the side of the van.' She looked into Sandra's unresponsive, upraised face and said impatiently, 'In the petrol station, stupid, where we waited for that first hitch. The van came in and the driver went into the office and I saw *it*,' her voice gloated.

'You mean you just – took it?' Sandra couldn't say the word 'steal'. She was glad she hadn't. The ghost-pale face held contempt, impatience, anger.

'Of course, idiot. Don't you want any souvenirs yourself of this summer?'

The deep whisper went on, speaking of past summers.

Sandra asked, 'Doesn't anyone complain? Say that something has – '

'Why should they?' Peta sounded honestly surprised. 'They're only small things. For Pity's sake, S. Kilby. Cafés *expect* to lose things, like hotels expect to lose towels and ashtrays and whatever. I just bet World Wide Novelties have a real stock of these.' Her hands caressed the little mascot again. 'They'd expect people to souvenir them. I just hope, that's all, that no one else I know gets one and takes the shine off this for me. Don't you' – the deep voice pressed impatiently – 'want souvenirs for yourself?'

Sandra stood up. She slipped back to her own bunk. She whispered across the space between them. 'Not that way.'

'And I get the horrors wondering what you're up to,' Sandra

said the next morning. They'd put the clown's costume and their underwear through the laundromat and were seated on high stools the other side of the drying machines, sipping coffee that tasted to Sandra like burnt cork.

She said as much, then again, because Peta hadn't answered, 'I get the horrors.' Almost apologetically she added, 'My parents would just about drop dead if I ever took so much as one single thing and – '

'*Saint* Kilby!' The deep voice mocked, then said, off-handedly , 'If it worries you you can say goodbye. I told you, you know' – her gaze followed the slop of coffee from the suddenly agitated cup in Sandra's hand – 'that there was no obligation either side.'

'I *like* having you around.' Her sudden smile flashed out. 'You're quiet, and I talk all I darn well like. If there were two of us talked like I do, we'd be screaming at one another in no time, and at home if I talk too much my step-dad gives me a look, so all right, on vacation I just have to talk or burst, and you're so quiet, so I like being with you, but I'm not going to let you spoil my fun. That's all it is, *Saint* Kilby. Just fun. Everyone does it and like I said last night, people *expect* you to souvenir.'

She slid from the stool. She asked, 'Are you coming? If not, the best place for picking up a ride is outside a petrol station, but chum up with the petrol filler. They'll chase you out otherwise. Some of them are too surly for living. If you chum up with one he'll put you wise to the drivers that might prove awkward. They can line them up exactly from the way they act. The no-tipper and the mean-tippers and the "get moving, you" type are no good, and they'll give you a tip about too much smell of drink, or a lot of bottles in the back. If you're lucky they'll actually ask what seems a decent ride to take you along and save you the job of even asking.'

Just an hour before Sandra had been determined to go on herself, she didn't want the parting to happen. She thought of approaching a service station worker, of being appraised, of trying to be friendly, all of her own accord, without Peta's clown-costume to break the ice.

There was a coach across the street. The passengers were getting out and going into the coffee shop. Silently, Sandra watched them, not even listening now to Peta's flow of advice. She was thinking of joining the coach, becoming part of that blank-faced group of people the other side road, and depression came to sit on her shoulder with so heavy a load she knew she couldn't leave.

She wanted to go on with Peta and hitch rides and laugh and chatter and be drawn by Peta into groups at the hostels. She didn't have to souvenir herself. She said abruptly, 'I want to come with you.'

The other girl shrugged. 'It's fine by me, just so long as you don't come the holier-than-thou, Saint Kilby. I won't stand for that. Get that?' Tossing Sandra's things to her she began stuffing her own into her rucksack. She said briskly, 'We want a ride straight west this time. That's the prettiest way over the mountains.'

She gained her objective with no trouble at all. As on the previous day the clown's absurd costume pulled up a car almost at once, but just as quickly, after a brief look at the driver, Peta was walking on, ignoring the slow pursuit of the car.

'Not that one. He's got two separate bashes and one's older than the other. Two separate smashes that is, and he's not insured or he'd have them fixed.' She waved the car on. 'See, Saint Kilby,' she mocked, 'how I'm educating you to the life of the road?'

The next car she took. Sandra was bundled into the front seat beside the woman driver, while Peta took the back. It was only a short hitch, but all through it Sandra sat taut. When they were on the road again she let the words spill out, 'Did you take anything?'

'No, dear Saint.' Peta slitted her eyes in sudden temper, then relaxed and laughed. 'You're a terrible idiot. You don't get souvenirs in cars, except just sometimes, like once' – her grin widened – 'there was this silly old goat. He got out at a petrol station and I had a look in the glove box and there's this real dirty book. I took that.' She giggled. 'I bet the old goat had fits for a week wondering if his wife had found it, or I had.' Then she shrugged impatiently, 'In cases like that, well, that's different, but otherwise there'd be only stuff like cash and cigarette cases and lighters. You can't touch that sort of thing. They'd raise the roof and, if you're caught, it's steal-ing and you're in real trouble.'

Sandra was to realise there was a sharp distinction between theft and the taking of things like the small plastic shell ash-tray, stamped with the name, 'Shell's Inn', from the restaurant where they were treated to tea by the two women who gave them their next drive west, leaving them on the plains, with the mountains a blue haze of shadow behind them.

Peta asked, and her voice held something close to pity for Sandra's future, 'Don't you want something to remind you of this summer? When I hold this' – she touched the little ash-tray – 'it'll all come back – all those gum trees and the little artificial waterfall and the smell of newly cooked scones and the beamy red face of the older of those two women and the way she called us both "dear" and I'll have all the enjoyment all over again.' Then she shrugged, 'Oh well, please yourself, Saint Kilby.'

Rain spoiled the next morning. A grumbling procession left the hostel, 'like cellophane wrapped parcels' as Peta put it, as they followed the long line of gaily coloured plastic macin-toshes down the grey road.

There was one thing about her companion, Sandra thought. Rain didn't damp her spirits or sour her sense of fun. Half of the crowd that morning had been surly and complain-ing of the rule that made travellers leave the hostels by nine, wet or fine, but Peta strode through the mud with her brown face uplifted to the rain as though she revelled in it, though she protested at Sandra saying so with, 'Not revel. It's a change though and we mightn't see rain again the whole trip. It'll be hard to hitch today. I can't dress up and drivers won't stop in rain. We'd mess up the cars with muddy boots and wet macs. We'll try one of the service stations, clean up the mud, then see if we can sweet-talk the men into letting us sit in the office while they fix us a hitch.'

Sandra knew real gratitude to the other girl as later they drove in the dry warmth of a station wagon, past straggling groups of figures who turned hopefully with upraised hand, only to let the hope slide away and the hands fall as they saw the car was full up. The elderly driver shook his head as he slowed to pass a group slogging through a stretch of water. 'There's too many of you on the roads these days,' he admonished. 'I told mother a fortnight back I wouldn't stop for any of you – there's just too many.' Then he smiled into the driving mirror where he could see them reflected in the back. 'I said to that chap in the petrol station, "No fear. No hitchhikers," but when I saw you – he said we'd laugh and so we did. A clown, now – ' He shook his head. Then he demanded, 'How are you going to get on in that rig when we turn you out on the road, young lady?'

'I was hoping you wouldn't,' Peta coaxed. 'Wouldn't it be nicer if you dropped us in a town, by a coffee shop?'

His smile died. He said tartly, 'And treat you to a good lunch?' His pale eyes had creased into slits of suspicion in his round, full-cheeked face.

The elderly woman beside him murmured something, but Peta laughed. Her deep voice chided, 'No. We've sandwiches with us, but I'll have to change somewhere, and a coffee place will have a Ladies, and we can get a drink and a place to eat out of the wet.'

'Ah?' Half protestingly, against the rise of the woman's murmur, he said, 'Well, you can't blame us if we think there's a touch coming. It's because we were touched so much last summer, that I said we wouldn't give lifts again and why I said, "No hitchhikers" to the petrol chap. We did a trip down south and the whole way it was waving thumbs, and some of them asked out flat if we wouldn't like to treat them to food and that. Some of them went on as though we'd been given a big favour by them coming along with us. I don't say I'd ever approve of girls hitching rides anyway. Too much chance of them landing in trouble they can't handle. That's really why I picked you up – because of you being girls. It wasn't that get-up of yours. Oh, I laughed hard enough, but if you'd been a boy you could have stayed right where you were, but it doesn't seem right to me, two girls hanging round that sort of place – some of the chaps in those petrol stations are pretty tough customers.'

Peta said confidently, 'I can look after myself.'

His glance went to the mirror, summing her up. He said at last, 'Maybe. How about the other of you?' His hand jerked towards Sandra. Without waiting for an answer he asked, 'You two girls been friends for a long time? Schoolfriends?'

Sandra was going to answer, and even, with the ice broken, tell him that this was the great adventure of her life, when from the back came Peta's silencing, 'We're friends of long standing.'

'And why did you say that?' Sandra asked later, watching Peta skim the clown's striped silk from her thin figure.

Peta laughed, 'Because I felt like a pun. Maybe though, considering the way we've had rides, I should have said friends of long *sitting*. Didn't you see for yourself he was looking for something to be righteous about? Tell him we'd met up on Central and he'd have been rampaging about the evils of going round with people you know nothing about. They do, you know.' She shrugged herself into the checked shirt and went over to the mirror of the coffee shop washroom to tidy her hair. 'The old goats like to feel shocked at the goings-on of flaming youth.' Her smile mocked at Sandra from the glass. 'I never let them. They get deadly boring. Didn't you notice how neatly I turned him into talk of last summer? His trip was interesting. They looked like a couple of real old stodges, but they proved interesting.'

'I liked them,' Sandra said slowly.

Peta gave a final upward flick to the ends of her brown hair. 'So, all right, I did, too, but why so solemn about it, my dear Saint?'

'I liked them too much to want them thinking badly about us.' The words exploded with a force she hadn't meant to use. 'You took something from that basket!'

Peta said crisply, 'Sometimes, Saint Kilby, you're a flaming bore!'

Without answering the question she strode towards the door, pushed it open and was beyond it before Sandra could grabble her own things together and follow. When she did it was to find Peta seated at a table in the shop, in a corner that gave her a view of the rainswept world outside. She didn't turn her head when Sandra sat down opposite, but went on staring out, apparently quite oblivious of everything except the rain and a sad, wet brown dog shivering outside.

When the sole waitress finally crossed the otherwise empty room to them, Peta said, still without turning, 'Coffee. Fresh coffee. I'll send it back, if not. Cream. Two doughnuts, if they're today's.'

The woman was obviously as tired as her creased blue uniform, her voice as dreary as the day, as she intoned, without expression, 'Coffee, cream, doughnuts.' Her pale-eyed stare fixed itself on Sandra in mute enquiry.

'Oh . . . the same, I think. Yes, of course, I'll just have the same.' When the woman had gone, she ventured, furious at herself with the timidity, the apologetic tone of her voice, when she was the one who had the right to be angry, 'Where are we going next?'

Peta turned. Her dark blue eyes were cold. She said crisply, 'I ought to retort to that,"*You* can go to the devil, Saint Kilby." I really ought. Perhaps I won't, though.' Abruptly she smiled. 'So, all right, you got my goat and I got mad, but it was your own fault. I told you flatly if you didn't want to come along with me, you needn't, and you said you wanted to and that meant you were going to turn a blind eye to taking souvenirs, if you were too saintly to play yourself.' Her arms went wide again in a gesture of exasperation, 'Then what do you pull? Babbling at me about maybe that old pair not liking us. What's it matter? We'll never meet up again.'

She settled back in her seat as the waitress dumped crockery and coffee on the table top. She said sharply, 'Wait on now,' and lifted the thick white cup, sipping the coffee, savouring it and then nodding. 'That's really good,' she said, but the woman seemed totally disinterested. Satisfied she had dealt with them, she went across to the far window, to gaze out too at the rain and the sad, wet dog.

Peta said, 'We'll try for a hitch outside here. If they see we're clean and dry we might be lucky. If not, we slog. There's a hostel not so far off the crossroads. You can check in any time after one and in this we might as well call it a day. All right by you?'

'Yes.' She didn't want to ask the question and perhaps be treated to that withdrawn silence again, but her lips formed the words and they spilled out in a blurted, urgent, 'Peta, what did you take off them?'

Peta sighed, then she gave a jerk of laughter. 'Why ever ask if the subject pains you? You're a real twit, but all right, if you must know – '

There was a flick of her hand, a tinkle, a glitter of light on silver. Sandra stared in real dismay, but the deep voice said placidly, 'It's not valuable. It's just polished-up cheap metal, the sort you get in those fifty cent dress rings from Woolworths, but it's unusual and really pretty.' With a shrug of her thin shoulders she added, 'She deserved to lose it anyway. She could've lost her purse and cash if I'd been a thief. She had the purse right there on top of the basket between us with the top gaping on the bulge of stuff she'd poked in, and she was so busy listening to what "Dad" – don't you *loathe* the way old folks call each other Mother and Dad? I'm never, never going to let my husband sink to that. Well, she was listening to *him* and you could see her saying to herself what a bright spark he was and she was being so pleased about that I could have taken anything. It's just as well for her I just wanted a souvenir of the hitch. This was right on top.' One brown finger touched the little pill box with its shape of a rose. 'It's real cute, isn't it?'

To agree might sound as though she acknowledged Peta's right to it, Sandra thought confusedly, yet to say nothing was going to see that she condemned again and she was frightened of Peta's temper and of her withdrawn silence.

She blurted out at last, conscious that the dark blue gaze was fixed on her, 'It's a pill box. What if she wants those pills and – '

Peta's brown hands flicked back the top. She shrugged, 'It's aspirin, or something.' She touched the round white tablets with a dismissing gesture. 'Look at the little mirror in the top. That's real real good things since we started – that shell and the little globe of the world, and this. I guess from now on I'll never get a worthwhile one. Any more'd be too much. Haven't you noticed if you ever have a real run of good luck there's always something bad follows it up? I'd be scared of any more luck. Oh, you can giggle if you like.' She slipped the rose shaped box into the pocket of her shirt. 'Can't you eat more that one crumb at a time, dear Saint? I was so hungry I could've munched the plate. I thought after all that chit-chat with the old pair they'd treat us. That was *his* doing. He gave me a look that said, "I told you so – no treats from me." So all right, they were interesting, but they were mean.'

She repeated the words in the almost deserted dormitory that night.

They had spent most of the evening speculating over what had happened to everyone else. Only a few others had arrived, dripping wet and morose, and struggling with the start of the flu. None of them had been part of the previous evening's crowd, and all of them had been tired, chilled and depressed by the unrelenting downpour outside and the day's dearth of lifts.

'I wasn't' – Peta said softly in the dormitory – 'going to let on how nicely we managed. They'd have guessed I had some gimmick and they'd have pried till they found it.' She suddenly chuckled, a slow deep warm sound of comfortable amusement. 'That last hitch did you ever see a sourer face? He didn't want to take us. If he'd been game he'd have dumped us as soon as we were clear of town. It was lucky that, going into the grocer's and having him there, a commercial, and saying out loud where he was going. He couldn't say no, we couldn't come along, too, with all of them listening and the rain teeming down outside, but his *face!*' She suddenly giggled and confessed, 'I paid him out anyway. I took his order book.' As Sandra shot up in the bunk beside her, she added comfortably, 'He'll just think he left it somewhere, but it'll make him run in circles, and it serves him right. He was sour. And that other chap, old "Dad" as she called him, he was interesting, but he was mean-natured.'

3

'I can remember Albert Bossley clearly.' The sun was shining through the slatted venetians on to Marion's face, but she didn't try moving. She was glad of that small shaft of warmth. She had crossed her long legs, linking her hands around her knees. She stared down at them as she added, her voice half puzzled, 'It's a ridiculous point, but out of it all I remember him best. Maybe it's because later on there was that terrible interview on television – do you remember?' She lifted her gaze then let it fall back to her linked hands.

'It doesn't matter. All I can remember of that I've put down in there,' she nodded to the folders of papers in front of Jefferson Shields. 'He came to the inquest, too, though he wasn't asked to give evidence. They adjourned if you know – twice, and there wasn't ever much evidence offered except the girls' statements and – the doctor, the medical evidence.

'Someone – I've forgotten now who it was – pointed Bossley out to me at the inquest. He was such an insignificant little man!' Her voice rose in shocked memory, then she coloured, because the man opposite was so insignificant. She said hastily, 'That sounds ridiculous, as though it would have made me feel better to find that he was tall and imposing, dramatic, something of that type.

'It was just – he didn't seem the type to rant and to rave and to insist the girls be picked up and to start the real tragedy rolling, right down to Jack's death, because he did, you see.

He went to the police about that little pill box. Oh, he had a right to be angry, but if he hadn't started the search for them, none of the rest of it would have happened. Isn't that incredible to reflect on?' Her gaze was wide and startled on his, then dropped away again.

'He was short. Very short. His face was quite big, but he was a small man, with white hair. It had been ginger once. There were ginger hairs on the backs of his hands. He sat quite close to me at the inquest. He kept looking at me and trying to catch my eye – I don't know why – and I didn't want to do it, so I kept looking down, and his hands were right there where I couldn't avoid them.

'Well, he went to the police. It's all in there,' she nodded to the stack of folders again.

'The police asked how he could be positive the girls had taken the box – that it just might have been lost somewhere and he told them it had been a test.' Gravely she added, 'I don't think that was fair. He put temptation in their way, or rather, Mrs Bossley did.

'You see, they'd been robbed the previous summer by hitch-hikers. He was still angry about that. There, in that service station that summer four years ago, he refused to take the girls. Mrs Bossley urged him to do it. She told him he was an old grudge-pot. She told him she'd prove to him that he was being too harsh. She said she'd leave the basket and her purse in the back and she was certain that when the girls left them everything would be intact.'

She lifted her gaze again. 'Do *you* think she was right to do that?'

'Perhaps not. Perhaps he agreed, to have the chance to prove his wife wrong. Was he that type?'

She smiled for the first time, little lines crinkling round her eyes. 'You *do* understand. Yes, I think he was the very type who always wanted to be right, so he took them.

'They were dropped at that café. Mr and Mrs Bossley never saw them again. They drove away, and out on the road

Mrs Bossley reached for the basket. The pill box was gone. Albert Bossley always claimed that it was the shock and disappointment that made her ill. Perhaps that's so. She certainly did get ill, and she didn't have her pills any more, and it's a fact that they only reached a doctor and hospital fast enough to save her life.'

Jefferson Shields moved slightly. He sad mildly, 'So he had a very good reason for extreme anger.'

'Yes. I've already admitted that, but – he was vicious. Not just angry. Vicious about it. He wanted them found and suitably punished and what suited his own ideas of punishment, too. It made him more angry still when the police told him that there wasn't much the law would do to them – that it would be treated as a stupid prank and perhaps they might be put on a bond. They certainly wouldn't be gaoled.

'Inspector Podmore maintains that Bossley wasn't a hard man, merely a shocked and angry one who would have calmed down in the end and seen reason, and he would have dropped charges when he had realised the publicity could spoil the girls' future.' She stopped. She shook her head. She said quite definitely, 'I think the Inspector was wrong. There, at the questioning at the inquest, Bossley wasn't upset or sorry for Jack or the girls, for anything at all. He wanted – I am quite sure of it – for us to compare notes, to share anger at the girls, to – well, rant about them. I think, but perhaps I'm not being quite fair, or accurate; perhaps I'm leading you astray. Inspector Podmore talked to him and had a chance – lots of chances – to weigh him up and decide what he was really like. I'm prejudiced perhaps, because I saw him first on that television interview. He was ranting. It's the only word.

'I couldn't forget that when I saw him in court, so perhaps I read a lot into his gazing at me that wasn't there at all.

'Perhaps he would have eventually done nothing, but he did do something – at first, and once the police realised that the girls had a very dangerous drug in their hands, that they might think was just aspirin – well, they considered it best to find them.'

Marion leaned forward to accept that cigarette that was silently offered her.

She said slowly, 'If they'd been quicker, if they'd found them at once – ' then she shook her head, pushing the pointless visioning aside.

'Albert Bossley couldn't describe them very well. I remember every word in his statement about them. He said' – her voice dropped and hardened – '"The tall one was all frogged up such a way I couldn't tell much about her except that her face was thin. Sunburned, too, but with that false red nose – it wasn't a girlish face, or one you could describe reasonably. The other was small and fair. She had a plait. It was hanging down the back of her jacket, tied with a bit of red ribbon."'

Marion leaned back. She smoked in silence and was grateful that he didn't speak or try to make her go on. At last she said, 'The great pity was that he couldn't tell some things and he made a mistake about others. One was about Peta's name.

'He saw the name on her rucksack, but either he misremembered, or he never saw it properly. He gave it to the police as Winchely, not Wincham, and he also told the police that the girls were old friends. That was Peta's doing, of course, but it was another error.

'He couldn't remember the name of the teashop either, or even the name of the town where he had left them. So you see' – there was regret in her voice, pain in her eyes then – 'the police had to find the teashop first, to find out where they went to afterwards. There was one delay after another. They never found them till the whole tragedy had worked itself out to the end.'

{ 4 }

They found the coffee shop easily. Although Albert Bossley hadn't remembered the name of the town, there were few towns at all between Moori, where Jan Bossley had been taken to hospital, and Pennants Crossing where the coffee shop, shuttered and dark, stood on the corner in the full drive and bitterness of the downpour at ten-fifty that night.

As other local constables in each town were doing, Constable Freed knocked at the shuttered door, and kept knocking, tirelessly, imperatively, as the flat upstairs remained dark and unresponsive.

He stood as tirelessly in the full slant of rain, as light finally came on and a window was raised. The woman's voice held alarm and shock. He soothed that first and put the question that was being put in all other towns on the way to Moori. The answer was given in tones thickened by a heavy cold, 'I haven't been in the shop all day, I've been so sick. There's never much doing when there's rain like this, so I left it to the waitress. That's Jessie Birkmyre. You ought to know as much yourself.'

He gained the address in spite of her arguments and it was only eleven-thirty when he reached the darkened house in a street beyond the shopping centre. He stood on the porch, index finger to the bellpush, wondering what the two girls had done, and why their movements were under scrutiny, wishing, as he had often wished in the past, that he could sometimes learn the full reasons for what he was doing, before he read about it in the press.

When there was still no answer, he circled the house, noted the locked windows, and came back to the porch, searching then for milk bottles. There weren't any, only a note, held by half a brick, on the porch floor, with a scrawled note, 'Visiting overnight. Leave two bottles tomorrow.'

The porch was sheltered from the downpour. He stood there, lighting a cigarette, debating whether to rouse the neighbours and question where Jessie Birkmyre was visiting.

He decided against it. Even if he knew, it was going to be after midnight before he found her. She'd be cranky and sharp-tongued for a certainty and entirely uncooperative. They always were when roused from sleep, and she'd be at the shop in the morning for a certainty, with the owner ill.

That point decided, he told himself comfortably that it was plain sense to leave seeing her till morning. She would be willing to talk all he liked then, he thought in wry amusement – they always were if it was on the boss's time and not their own.

{ 5 }

SANDRA

The sun was back. That was Sandra's first knowledge when she woke. A bright slant of it was coming full on her face through the uncurtained dormitory windows. She rolled over, trying to escape, and saw the face of the clock. It seemed unreasonable that the sun was fully up and the world awake before five, and she closed her eyes again, ignoring the rustlings from the other bunk that told her Peta was awake, too. Later, drifting towards sleep again, she heard the deep voice speaking to her, but she refused to answer, then abruptly she was wide awake, staring upwards in real temper, because she had been wrenched from comfort and peace with a violent shaking.

She blinked, stared and half rose. She demanded, 'What is it?' in something close to panic because she had never seen Peta look that way before, thin-lipped, with two bright circles of red high on her cheek bones, as though she had decided on clownish make-up to go with her costume.

Only Peta wasn't yet dressed as a clown. Sandra became aware at the moment that she realised Peta was already fully dressed, and that her rucksack, strapped and buckled, was ready at her side.

Sandra asked again, 'What is it?'

'You going to sleep all day?' The question came almost violently, the deep voice roughened and cracked.

A glance at the clock face brought an outraged, 'All *day*! just look at the time!'

Peta gazed, blank-faced. In the same oddly roughened voice she said, 'The sun rose long ago. I'm ready to go. We'll breakfast somewhere outside. Why not? This place stinks – the kitchen, I mean. It's been shut up all night. It stinks. Of last night's cooking and everyone's got a cold. They're all moaning and sniffling. If we stay around we'll be catching wogs. You want to spend the rest of your holiday toting Kleenex and a cold in the head?'

Her voice went on pressing and urging and ordering. Sandra wasn't proof against it. She found herself being hustled through showering and dressing and packing, and running after Peta's long strides as the older girl made for the front door.

Even on the road, Peta didn't slacken. Her lithe, long strides carried her too quickly for Sandra's comfort, but even when she protested, Peta said only, 'I'm hungry. I want to find shops.'

Sandra stopped, in mid-stride. She pointed out in temper, 'They'll be closed at this hour. Why on earth did you drag me away like this?'

'There'll be something open, for the truckies. If I remember right there's a petrol station with a restaurant along here a bit. A truckies' pull-in. There'll be food and lots of it. I could eat a horse.'

She stopped, staring back at her companion, her dark blue eyes narrowing. 'You ever thought, Saint Kilby, that you look like a horse yourself? With that plait down your back, I mean. You remind me of one of those horses at the Easter Show, with their tails plaited up. I always get really irked at that, it's so unnatural and, for love's sake, what's wrong with a tail as it is? It looks silly in a plait. So does your hair.'

There seemed nothing to say that mightn't start a quarrel, Sandra thought helplessly. Peta's bright spirits, her sense of fun, seemed to have been swept away with the night's deluge. This was a new Peta – someone with a hard, tart tongue, deliberately trying to make trouble.

Why? Sandra wondered, and then Peta smiled and her voice seemed less roughened and cracked when she said, 'Well, all right, so I've got a hide. Haven't I? I can see in your face you're bottling up a lot of things to say back. So all right, I got out of bed the wrong side. I did. All night it was coughing and snivelling all round me and I couldn't sleep with the racket and I got mad just lying there and seeing you sound asleep when I couldn't go off myself.'

She eyed the other girl thoughtfully, 'Just the same, why not let your hair loose? It's not so long. You looked real pretty last night when you had it loose on your shoulders, and your hat'd keep it off your face. You'll get dust in it no matter what you do, so why look like a horse?'

Only for a moment did Sandra think of resistance. It was a small point and if it was going to put Peta in a sweet temper again there was plenty in favour of it. Standing there at the side of the road she undid the plait, combing the strands smooth. She said, meeting Peta's dark gaze and wondering at the look that was almost excitement, 'I never wear it this way. It's thin. Too thin to have loose. It looks thick in the plait, but it isn't. It looks straggly.'

'It looks different.' Again Sandra knew puzzlement at the satisfaction in the words, but then Peta was turning, back to the sun again, heading down the dusty grey road to the west, calling over her shoulder, 'Put a spurt on, Saint Kilby – I'm starving. I really am.'

She was still edgy though. She insisted on taking a back table in the restaurant and she studiously ignored the friendly 'Mornings' offered by the few truckies present.

She said, when they'd ordered, 'They get fresh if you let them. You remember that,' but her almost violent rejection of an offer to let her have a look at the morning paper was a complete reversal to the thin-lipped, roughened-voiced character of the early morning.

Meeting Sandra's gaze she abruptly grinned. She said, 'What'd I want with the news? You tell me. I can tell you it all myself. Someone's on strike and someone else is murdered, and there were umpteen dozen car crashes in the last twenty-four hours, and the Minister for Transport says something will have to be done to stop this slaughter on the roads. My step-father says every minister has said that at least once a week since horses went out and cars came in. Don't you like sausages?'

'Yes.' Sandra stopped poking hers, and swallowed a mouthful, but the day seemed to have lost half its sunshine. Peta in this mood was difficult – too difficult for comfort, or pleasure.

She asked at last, 'Would one of these men take us?'

'I wouldn't accept. They're not supposed to have passengers anyway, but I wouldn't ask. Or accept. Some of them are real sneaky. They get somewhere and then accuse you of swiping their wallets. What can you say? No matter what, they just laugh and it's police and the lock-up for you or a nice bit of fun for them under the trees.' She shook her head. 'You're terribly green, Saint Kilby. You'd be altogether lost and in trouble in no time without me.'

Sandra was thinking the same. The reminder put paid to any idea of trying to say goodbye, of shouldering her pack and simply walking in the opposite direction to Peta and not meeting up with her again. Temperament and edginess and all, she had to put up with Peta or start taking coaches – that was all there was to it.

Resignedly she followed Peta outdoors. Even at a little past seven there were cars on the road, but Peta strode on without trying to thumb any of them down, though her quick head-turn as each came up and past raked over the car and driver.

'What are you waiting for?' Sandra demanded at last, stopping, but Peta went on walking. Only when she realised that she wasn't being meekly followed did she stop and turn. She called sharply, 'Hurry up!' but Sandra stood still. She demanded again, 'What are you waiting for? We could have had a lift by now.'

Peta said flatly, 'They had radios and had them going. I've got a headache. If you want to know it feels like seven sledge-hammers.'

Sandra felt a sweet relief. A headache was something reasonable, and something understood and to be sympathised with. It gave promise that in a few hours Peta would revert to her usually gay self. She hurried to catch up. She said anxiously, 'I wish you'd said before what it was. Why didn't you take some aspirin there in the café?'

'I hate it. I hate all drugs!' There was something near to violence in the answer. Peta half turned, gaze searching the oncoming car. Then she lifted her hand and walked calmly into the road, so the car was forced to stop.

She faced up to the frowning woman with a soft, 'I wouldn't have pulled you up that way, only I feel just terrible. I've a headache you could – '

The woman said tartly, 'It's amazing how walking brings on headaches. You're the fourth in a week with the worst headache in the world. It *is* the worst in the world, isn't it?' Impatiently she leaned back to throw open the rear door. 'Oh, get in – but frankly you kids are a darn nuisance. Where are you going?'

'West.' Peta sank into the seat and closed her eyes.

'Just west? Nowhere in particular, just west? All right then. You can tell me when to stop or I'll put you off near the farm.'

She seemed as content as Peta not to talk, and Sandra made no effort to break the silence. She was near to sleep when the car finally stopped and the woman turned to say, 'End of the road, kids.'

With both of them grabbing at their packs she asked softly, 'And now, before you go, just what've you taken out of the back there? You can get out and wait while I look.'

Sandra stared, white-faced, only moving when Peta's hand thrust hard into her back, almost sprawling her on to the road. Peta said quietly, 'We've touched nothing. We'll wait while you see.'

There were two boxes. The woman opened both. Then she stood hesitating. She said at last, 'Well, I'm ashamed. I probably look it, and I certainly feel it, but there's been trouble, and I had the idea you might be the two who'd caused it.' Meeting

Peta's blank eyes she shook her head. 'I expect you've not seen the morning paper? Have a look at it later. I thought – I was testing you, really, but the names are wrong.' She nodded to their packs.

'I'm sorry. I do apologise. Here – ' Abruptly she thrust fruit into their hands, loading them till they could hold no more, then she jumped back into the car, waved to them, and turned the car on to a narrow side road off the highway.

Sandra stood staring at the fruit. She said, in wonder, 'What was all that about? She thought we were going to steal because of something, some trouble, in the paper – '

Now she remembered the almost violent refusal of the morning paper in the café. Anxiety touched her with raw flame, and she flared up, 'There was something in the paper you didn't want me to see! Wasn't there? You've been edgy all morning because something's wrong, and I mustn't know. I bet, I just *bet*' – her voice was rising – 'that you saw a paper at the hostel and – '

'Do be quiet.' Peta held tightly to the fruit. 'Come into the shade and pack this up and oh, all right, so there was something bad and so I was edgy and got into a panic. Like I said, I couldn't sleep last night and the sun got up and so I did, too, and I sneaked down and there was this paper on the step with the crate of milk and there wasn't anyone about to say I couldn't read it, so I did and there was this story. See, I made a mistake, and you've no right to stare at me like that!' The red circles of flame were back in her high cheekbones. 'I made a mistake. People do. Make mistakes. This was mine.'

'What, in particular?'

'That box. That little pill box. It was valuable. I made a mistake about that. Now there's a fuss, but I wasn't to know.' Her hand shot out and the fruit spilled into the dust, but she didn't notice it. Her fingers were gripping tightly to Sandra's arm. 'You *know* I wouldn't have got us into trouble.'

When there was no answer she went on rapidly, 'I was that sick I nearly threw up. All I could think about was us getting away before the hostel matron woke up and saw that paper or some of the others did, though they didn't see that box. No one did. Except you, but I thought – '

Sandra said sharply, 'That woman in the car said something about our names being wrong.'

She watched the thin brown hand shoot out to cover the name tag on the grey canvas, then it fell away. Peta said flatly, 'I took it off. The one that said Wincham. I took this one off my jacket and sewed it on to cover the space because it was my own name – Squire. So, all right, I took the first one off. the old woman saw it wrongly anyway, or got muddled or forgot. The paper said Winchely, but I was scared.'

Sandra sat staring at the spilled fruit in the dust. It was a long time before she said, 'You wouldn't take a lift in any car with a radio. You were scared the radio would say what the paper did, and I'd know about it.' She lifted her gaze to the thin brown face. 'I had a right to know, and you couldn't have hidden things for ever.'

'So what if you'd read it there in the hostel?' The blue eyes were angry and bitter. 'You with your silly saintly conscience! You'd have had hysterics maybe and blurted the whole thing out. Or there in the café – I can imagine you screeching and spilling your breakfast. Or on the road, with it coming over the radio – don't be a twit! I had to get you alone to tell you and make you see sense.'

'About what?'

'About a mistake being something no one can help. I couldn't help it, but you'd have gone blurting out it was me took it, for a certainty, and no one's to know.' Her voice was roughened and cracked again. 'Not ever.' Her hand reached out, shaking at Sandra's arm. 'You're the only one who knows, and you're the only one who can tell about that clown suit. You're not going to!'

When there was still no reply, she shook Sandra's arm again. 'No one's going to know!'

Sandra said slowly, 'They seemed nice. If you went – does

the paper give their name? – well if you went to them and gave them the box and explained, I don't think they'd do anything much except talk to us – '

Peta started to laugh. She hugged her thin arms round her upraised knees and rocked with the force of it. Through it the words stuttered into the hot air, 'You're sure of – of that?' Then she sobered. She said, 'Wash that idea right out. They've set the police on to us, haven't they? That means they're good and mad. From now on we'll be like two little mice, Saint Kilby. I shan't wear my clown rig any more.' Her voice held regret for that fact. 'And you look different altogether with your hair out of that horse plait, and the name on my pack's different. Just to be safe though we won't use the hostels any more. Oh, I know, there's never talk of surnames or anything but just your Christian name, but someone might've noticed the name on my pack and your horse plait and started thinking. They *might* be able to put a name to us!' At Sandra's startled jerk she jeered, 'Ah, now you're scared! There's not much chance of it, but I don't want to sit around every evening and having to listen to everyone talk about that blessed pill box. It was just a mistake.'

She fell into a brooding silence, broken at last by, 'We can put up at farms. If we offer to pay and show we've money they'd probably put us up just for a bit of help with washing up. A farmer's wife always likes an extra pair of hands.'

'I don't want them to be mine.' At Peta's glance, Sandra added, 'I don't mean I object to washing up. I just object to being in this mess.' She couldn't bring herself to add a blunt, 'Go away, I don't want to be mixed up in it. The trouble is yours, not mine,' but the words were there, unspoken between them.

Peta said, 'You'd tell on me.'

'No, I won't.' Sandra had bent, taking the fruit from the dust, brushing it clean with her small hands.

Peta's hand reached out, drawing her upright in a determined grip. 'And what if someone did see our names in the hostel last night, or the night before, and they put Christian names to us and *you're* picked up. That old chap could identify you. I was a clown. He'd have a hard job saying I was me, but you – you were clearly enough seen. What would you say if you were picked up?' The clasp tightened.

It was no use getting into a panic. Sandra told herself that, but panic was making a hard tight knot in her throat and tightening a band of pain round her head. She said at last, 'That I didn't know about you taking things and that when I did we went off in different directions and I don't know where you are.'

Peta's voice was contemptuous, 'And of course you never ever knew my name, did you? Do you think you'd get away with playing that dumb?'

Sandra thought over that. She said at last, 'It's the way I suggested. We have to go to them and explain. Otherwise I just couldn't bear the thought we might be found and dragged out into the open like, like – criminals.' She added, 'My parents would just about drop dead! We'll have to go to those old people and you can explain you didn't know it was valuable, that you took it just for a silly prank and that – '

Peta's voice held that roughened, cracked note again. 'They won't listen.' The voice was suddenly muffled in the pressure of the thin brown hands hiding her face from the other girl. 'You said she might want those pills and she did. I said they were maybe aspirin. So, all right, I was wrong, but how was I to know? She nearly died because she didn't have them.' The hands fell away. Her voice strengthened to rage, 'How was I to know? She *let* me take them. She left that box right in front of me, and she's terribly sick and now he's set the police on us, and what do you think everyone's going to say to us if they find us?'

The fruit had fallen from Sandra's lap again. She said, 'Are you telling me everything *now*? Or is there something more – something worse?'

'No. It's quite bad enough. He must be furious, or he wouldn't have set the police on us. That means he won't listen, no matter how prettily we talk.'

In the silence between them there was the whisper of wind in trees, a faint rustle in undergrowth behind them, the quick impatient sound of a sparrow watching hopefully for food.

Finally Peta asked, 'Well, aren't you going to say something?'

After a long hesitation, Sandra shook her head. She wanted to say a lot, but all of it would have been futile and might only rouse Peta's temper. Peta said, 'There's hardly a chance in the world anyone'd connect us with it and say our names. Why should they? You're the only one knows I was the clown.' Her hand reached out. Her voice pleaded, 'I don't want to be on my own. I couldn't go off with anyone else and I have to have someone to talk to.'

Then she shook her head. She said flatly, 'So, all right, you needn't say anything. I can read your face. You don't want me around any more. So, all right, that's settled, but you just understand this, Saint Kilby. No one knows which of us took that box. You start bawling, and maybe I'll throw the blame right into your saintly lap. You understand?'

She looked down at the spilled fruit in the dust. 'We'll have to take this with us. That woman might see it otherwise and start wondering why we dumped it. It's good fruit, too.' She bent, slowly brushing the dust from each piece, stuffing them in to the canvas packs. 'We'll get the first lift possible to a place where there's a coach or train line. That's safest now. You stick to coaches and trains and maybe cheap guest houses and farms – any of the coach drivers would put you wise about places – and you won't have any trouble, not unless you start opening your mouth about me being that clown.'

{ 6 }

There had been no reluctance on Jessie Birkmyre's part to talk of the previous day. The difficulty had been to get her to stop, to sift through the maze of words and find something worthwhile to report.

That morning, Constable Freed had read the newspapers and had cursed the system that told him to do things without telling him why; cursed too, his leaving of the woman to the morning, though he had reminded himself that with luck the two girls, even if they'd been counting dollars and cents carefully enough to avoid buying newspapers, had seen the report and had known they were carrying with them a highly dangerous drug, even though the tablets looked like aspirin. Perhaps, he had reflected, going to the interview with Jessie Birkmyre, it would serve them right if they took one.

There was no doubt that they had taken the box. The flood of Jessie's comments made it plain that they had had it. She had seen it. It had been tossed on the table between the two girls. She had shown him the very same table and told him of seeing two girls leave the car and come running into the café, and her astonishment at having a clown sail in through the door.

'Oh, she had a manner, that one.' Jessie had soured the red plum of her thin lips over the remembrance. 'Where's the washroom?' she snaps at me and later she ordered off me as though she was talking to a dog.'

She had doubted that the girls were on really good terms. She told him that definitely, then amended it to, 'Not at first anyway. That clown one came out of the Ladies by herself, changed into a mac and jeans, all on her high horse over something, and the other crept out and tried smoothing her down.'

Regretfully she had to admit she hadn't known what they talked about, though she had tried listening, but the gurgle of water in downpipes, the beat of it on the iron awning outside the shop and the rush of it down the gutters had stopped her hearing.

She hadn't noticed the names on the packs either, but the smaller one had a long fair plait down her back. A peaked face, she thought, but her own face expressed doubt in the words. Just small and fair was all he said in the end – small and fair with a long plait down the back of her dark blue raincoat.

The other girl she described as tall and thin and dark – skin darkened by the sun anyway, she amended that. Her hair had been either short or screwed up out of the weather under a peaked weatherproof hat. The hat had been black and the coat bright yellow. She remembered that clearly.

She had seen them leave town, too. She was sure of that. She had been standing by the window again. There had been nothing to do except stare out at the weather, so she told him bluntly that she had seen the bright flash of yellow and seen both of them in the back of a small car. A man had been driving.

By ten Freed had reached the grocery store in his search for someone who, like Jessie, had had nothing to do but stare at the weather, and had seen the girls go by.

The fair one's name was Saint-something. Freed learned that from the pale-faced assistant, who whispered the information almost apologetically. Oh yes, she was sure, she nodded her head of pale hair vigorously. The girls had bought cooked meat, and the tall one had talked of not wanting to cook anything that evening, and she had looked over the biscuit display and had called to the fair one to ask if she fancied lattice biscuits.

'She called her name,' the whisper confided. 'She called, "Do you fancy lattice ones, Saint – " I didn't get what the rest was. I thought from that they were maybe nurses. My sister's a nurse. They call the other nurses just by their surnames. It sticks. My sister now – she calls her friends Parker and Lewis even outside. It sounds so odd.'

Freed thought over the information and dismissed it. Nurses, he was certain, would never have taken someone's tablets. He tried to remember what other sort of occupations there were where a girl might use a surname alone. The army, he remembered, but the girls sounded too young for that.

He was still thinking of that as he jotted down the rest. The girls had asked for a lift from Mr Donovan the traveller for Bridge Biscuits, and he had taken them. They were all sure of that. The girls had asked him to put them down at the youth hostel eight miles along the western road.

Their descriptions were vague. The girls had been wrapped up against the weather, but all of them remembered the fair plait of hair and the other's sun-darkened skin.

It was nearly eleven before he had contacted the youth hostel and the matron. She was curt and annoyed and told him forcibly she had had no time to look at anyone the previous day. Most of the young people had arrived with heavy colds and all had been drenched.

As for names, her laugh was caustic. They had long ago, she assured him, given up asking anyone to sign the visitors' book. They'd put down anything. If he liked to see them she had old books he could view. If he chose to believe the signatures, Elizabeth Taylor had been a frequent guest and so had the Queen, not to mention the Prime Minister and his wife.

No, she assured him, she hadn't noticed fair plaits, and sunburned skins were two a penny. Certainly some of the boys and girls might have known the two he was seeking and learned their names, but house rules were house rules – everyone had left by nine o'clock and had scattered she didn't know where.

Patiently Freed pored over the map, with the memory that

the girls had been heading west when Albert Bossley had picked them up and had still been heading west when they had gained a lift from the biscuit traveller. If they had break-fasted at the hostel they might have sought a lift – he stopped there and reached for the phone again.

The matron's voice was tarter than ever, but she answered promptly and definitely. Yes, she had the morning papers delivered and yes, they had been opened when she had come down to collect them and the day's milk, though that wasn't unusual. The young people grudged the coins for buying them. So long as they didn't make off with her papers alto-gether she never objected.

Not many bothered with a full breakfast, she explained to his other question, but that wasn't unusual either. It was more the boys who cooked in the morning. The girls made do with coffee and fruit.

No, she remembered that with obvious surprise now, there hadn't been a mention from anyone about the report in the paper. Yet her paper had definitely been read. She was quite sure.

So whoever had read it had left before the woman had come down and read it herself and perhaps started looking for fair plaits and the name of Winchely, Freed reflected in satisfaction. Before the other youngsters could hear the news and comment on it, too. Which meant the two had left without waiting to eat.

It was obvious where they might have gone, and in the truckies' café, as Freed expected, the waitress remembered them. The truckies had tried to be affable and the tall one had snapped at them – had refused the offer of a newspaper, too, and had been rude about it.

It had been that that had made her notice them. The place had been busy enough to keep her mind on the job. Of one thing she was sure. The girls hadn't tried getting a lift from any of the men.

'They were used to hitch-hiking.' The elderly woman shifted her weight from one knotted set of varicose veins to the other and sighed softly about it, her dark eyes glazed with the effort of memory. 'They were used to it. The first-time ones will jump at the chance of a truck ride. The men go such a long stretch at a time, you see, but some of the chaps see it just as a chance to play the fool with the girls. The ones who know about hitch-hiking steer clear of the trucks. I did wonder, the way the tall one slapped the men down, as if they'd had a set-to with a truckie just recently.' The tall girl had certainly been upset about something. She was definite about that. The other one – oh no, she was certain about that, too – had no plait. She had long fair hair with a bit of a curl to it, over her shoulders.

With all her efforts to remember, she couldn't tell him much more. They had been just girls, she smiled apologetically. The small one had had long fair hair, and she'd have called the face roundish. Oh no, not peaked. Small yes, but roundish, and, yes, now she came to think of it, a dimple in her chin. About fifteen was her guess at age. The tall one had had a brown skin and long straight dark hair and looked a bit older.

They hadn't hitched a ride from the men. They hadn't hung round outside either. The last she had seen of them they had been walking, not even waving to passing cars, and heading west again.

Back at the police station Freed waded through it all and sighed in dissatisfaction. They were still just vague figures, lost somewhere in the haze to the west. One was tall and sunburned with long dark hair and her name was Winchely, if Albert Bossley had remembered right. She might be dressed as a clown, but that was very doubtful now, after the press report. The other was about fifteen, with long fair hair. She had a round face and a dimple in her chin, and her name was Saint-something.

One thing was sure, though. They had read the paper now. They knew they possessed a dangerous drug, so they wouldn't touch it.

It hardly seemed worth the bother of further enquiries.

SANDRA

The name of the place was Asherton. Sandra sat on the green
park bench, her gaze on the pink blaze of Crepe Myrtle banked
before her, thinking of the name and wondering why it was
called that. It saved her from thinking of other things; saved
her, too, from having to turn and look at the girl beside her.

She wished Peta would go. She longed for that free-
swinging stride to take the tall, thin figure into the distance
till it became a speck and a shadow and then just a bad memory. Resentfully she picked at the memory of Peta saying
they'd hitch a ride to the nearest town with a coach line and
then part.

They had had the ride and it had brought them to town
and left them in the bright blaze of noon-day bustle, where
four grey roads met round a green-crusted, dried-out horse
trough relic of the past, and she had stood waiting, the sun
hot on her back through her thin blue shirt, for Peta to stride
away down one of those grey straight roads, so that she herself could take the opposite way.

Peta had simply stared at the trough, yet her gaze had
been oblivious of it and the traffic about them. Sandra had
turned away, towards the right and had stopped, the flame
colour of panic and temper rushing into her face, because
Peta had silently turned to follow.

She had asked, the rough edges of her voice tearing down the last vestige of friendship between them, 'What do you want?'

The heavy lids had closed over the bright blue gaze, then Peta said slowly, 'I guess, well, you didn't say goodbye.' The words were accusing.

Sandy had stared in astonishment. 'Why should I? We said – back there in the road – we'd take a lift and then we'd go in different directions. There wasn't anything else to say.'

'Except – a promise.' Peta's hand had clasped tightly to the younger girl's arm. 'Promise me you'll never say a word, never say to anyone, ever, that – ' she jumped at the harsh blare of sound close to them. 'Oh come away out of this! We'll be run over in a minute.' Her gaze swivelled, sought and fixed on distance. 'There's a park down there.'

Sandra hadn't wanted to go, but with Peta holding tight to her arm it had been go or make a scene, and in the park it was quiet and shady and the pink blaze of Crepe Myrtle was light in the shadows on her mind.

She went on wishing that Peta would go, but she didn't try breaking the silence between them. Any speech of her own was going to bring a flood of words from the other, she knew. She didn't want to listen to them, but she had to when Peta said slowly, 'I'm sorry for what I said. Back there in the road. I was so upset, you see, and you looked so *righteous*, and you sounded it, too, and all along you've needled me about what was just a prank and maybe I'd have stopped right off in the beginning, only you were so *righteous* and you kept sending me looks of pure agony when we were in cars, like you expected me to do something awful and just to needle you back. That was really why I took that little box. I saw you taking a long look at that open purse and then another look at my face as though you were just waiting for me to dip my fingers in. So I did, to spite you!

'I remembered that, back there in the dirt by the road, and I hated you, because I wouldn't ever have taken that box but for that. I didn't want it. Oh, it was pretty, but I didn't really want to take it. It was you looking at me in that fashion that needled me into needling you right back.'

Sandra pressed her fingers over her ears. She couldn't go on listening to the words repeated over and over, that were thrusting the blame at herself. She said, to drown them, 'What do they do to people who're caught doing things like that?' and then wished she hadn't, because the deep voice throbbed at her, 'I guess you go to gaol. Once the police start hunting you, you finish up there, if they catch you. What am I going to do with this?'

Sandra turned. Sunshine caught at the metal, outlining each edge of the rose-shaped top to the little box. It seemed to her that the other girl was trying to thrust the evidence on to her, as well as most of the blame.

She said in revulsion, starting up and away, 'Throw it away! Throw it away – quickly!'

She watched the metal arc in sun-caught brightness, to fall into the depths of the stone-edged pond by the Crepe Myrtles. The green-brown water rippled for only a few seconds and was still again, but before the last ripple had gone Sandra was hurrying away across the grass, willing herself not to look back to see if Peta was watching, or even following.

The children had welcomed the sun's return with delight and there had been no objections at all to them going to the park. The tears and the tantrums of a day cooped indoors because of the downpour outside had tried adult tempers to the limit.

Bronwyn was the youngest, and they didn't want her. At ten and eleven there were secrets for confidence and games to play where a seven-year-old wasn't welcome, especially a seven-year-old of matchstick thinness, her monkey gargoyle of a face ever ready to give pout-mouthed confidences to adults.

They could outrun her and did, though her thin legs and small feet in brown dusty sandals seemed tireless, so that she finally came up to them when they stopped.

'Go away, go away!' they chanted, and pushed and shoved her from their circle with a vigour that changed from exasperation to cruelty, leaving her finally alone and too bright-eyed.

'Go and play with the babies,' they'd flung at her and cropped dark head high she decided to do just that. If their mothers weren't around she could boss the babies because she herself had been bossed by her elders.

Sue Jack she knew. Sue's brown curls were to be seen every fine day behind the white picket fence of the corner house, and Sue's elder brother wanted no part of her that sun-filled day of the summer holidays. 'You look after her, kid,' he smiled winningly at Brownwyn, linking the hands of the two children. 'Bring her to the gates at one. We've got to go home then. You can see the tower clock anywhere in the park.' He demanded anxiously, 'You *can* tell the time, can't you?'

Bronwyn's contemptuous look dismissed him. It dismissed all opposition from the others she found, small flotsam left high and dry by exasperated elders.

She made a circle of them and made herself Queen and danced with them, follow-my-leader along arched green tunnels through the shrubbery, and out across the grass in the full sunlight, till they dropped exhausted in the shadow of the Crepe Myrtles. She was sick of them by then. She wanted to lie by herself and look into the green-brown water and just imagine things.

She paid no attention when the boy pulled off his sandals and edged dusty feet into the water, though her eyes calculated the depth of it, saw it didn't come beyond his grubby knees and was satisfied.

She ignored him. Somewhere in the green-brown there was a flash of red-gold, as a small fish passed by. She lay flat, face cupped in dusty hands, waiting for it to dart back. She ignored the children and their voices and even the clustering of them about the boy when he scrambled back to the grass.

Only when the dart of sunlight danced a silver shaft to the corner of her eye did she stop peering into the water in search of a glimmer of gold. She sat upright, gaze narrowed and angry. Her hand darted. 'Give *me* that!' she demanded and because her fingers were stronger than the boy's, she gained it.

He stood glaring at her, bullet head with its cropped dark hair thrust at her in anger, almost as big as herself, in spite of being three years younger.

He threw at her, '*You* didn't find it. My toes found it.' He wriggled them for her inspection.

She mocked, 'Toes can't find things, stupid. Toes haven't eyes and ears and brains.'

'They've *feels*!' he shrieked back at her, hands outstretched to pummel, but laughing, she danced out of reach, holding the little box high, laughing again in delight at its prettiness.

She told him scornfully, 'It's not a boy's box. It's a girl's. A silver box. A fairy box.' Staying carefully out of their reach she inspected it, delighting in its prettiness all over again, finding the catch and opening it.

They crowded to see. Their hands were outstretched to her. Maggie demanded, 'Sweeties?' with hope.

Suddenly apprehension, a remembrance of warnings, and her aunt's hands pressing the tiny catch of a gilt and enamel box as small as the one she held, flowed back to her, making her snap the box shut again.

At the two-year-old's pull on her dress, and the continued piping entreaty, she said impatiently, 'They're not sweets, stupid. They're pills. Fairy pills,' she elaborated to silence them and frighten them away. 'You mustn't touch them. If you do' – she sought for a threat so awful it would give her peace – 'if you do, you'll grow another pair of ears!'

She danced away, laughing, holding the silver box high so that the sunlight touched it and sparkled on it. They were still standing patiently waiting when she circled back. She knelt then to put the box into the pocket of the jacket she had dropped to the grass when they'd reached the pool.

They watched in stolid silence. Suddenly impatient with them, disgusted that she had to play with them, she turned her back and circled the pool, dropped down again, flat to the grass, with her face propped into her hands, staring once more into the green-brown water.

The boy squatted, watching her thoughtfully, a sullen silence holding him against the pulls and entreaties of the other children, till finally they left him and went dancing in and out among the Crepe Myrtles.

The box was his and he clung to the pleasure of his sullen anger against Bronwyn's grasping hands, but his anger held a calculated patience that kept him unmoving till he was sure she had lost consciousness to everything except her own dimmed reflection in the water. He eased himself flat then, and slid till his hand found her jacket, and the pocket and the box.

The others had danced right away. He slid into the shadow of the Crepe Myrtles, a pink spear brushing his cropped dark head and he inspected the box, pressing the tiny catch and staring at himself in the mirror in the lid.

The white tablets spoiled his pleasure in possession. He was afraid of them. Not because of Bronwyn's threat. She hadn't been able to hide her own amusement at it, he remembered, but because of the locked bathroom cabinet at home. It hadn't always been locked. Only a little while before he had been able to scramble up and open it and peer into the bottles. He hadn't yet forgotten the result – the angry voices and the stinging slaps and the shouted warnings of disaster that had flayed his ears.

In sudden revulsion against the memory he held the box upside down, watching the green grass flower with white circles. When he looked up it was to see the others had returned and that a circle of eyes were watching him, condemning his possession of the box.

He jumped up in alarm, thrusting it inside his shirt. He went running over the grass through the sunlight, feeling the pleasurable bump of the box against his body as he ran, a pleasure not even faintly dimmed by the knowledge that some of the children were running after him. He was confident of outdistancing them. He didn't so much as look back, or notice that Maggie, fascinated by the white circles she had hoped were sweets, had stayed behind, to reach out one hand and gently touch a circle and lift it.

Her hand closed protectively over it as Bronwyn's voice probed, 'What are you doing? Where are they all?' There was a piercing cry of real pain then. In anguished awareness Bronwyn stared at the white circles, and ran to her jacket and back, to scrabble in the grass at the pills.

'My box – he *took* it!' Grief shrilled her voice. 'I've lost it.'

In apprehension of her own possible loss Maggie lifted her hand and in smug triumph rounded her mouth over the white circle. She was amazed and disgusted at the bitterness that touched her tongue. She paid no attention to Bronwyn's jumping up and her angry scattering of the white circles over the grass before darting away. Maggie was too busy trying to rid her mouth of that bitter taste, but the sweet had fizzed and dissolved and she couldn't get rid of it at all.

{ 8 }

Marion hadn't been aware of a bell pressed, of orders given. She had thought him intent on the papers in front of him, but coffee and a saucer of sweet biscuits was silently placed in front of her.

She looked at them with revulsion. She turned, about to tell the elderly woman to take them away again, but the woman smiled at her. It was a singularly sweet smile that lifted the heaviness of her jawline and made her look younger.

The smile said, Drink it, as plainly as words had done.

Jefferson Shields said, 'Thank you, Mrs Dogsbody.'

The sweet smile touched Marion's face again. The woman went out silently. Marion blurted out, 'Is her name really Mrs Dogsbody?' Impatiently she added, 'I don't believe it.'

He smiled at her. For the first time she warmed slightly to him as he said, 'No one asked you to believe it, but I wanted to break your tension. You have been sitting so rigidly I found it painful. As you must have done. You know' – he sipped at the coffee, put down the cup and lifted the next folder – 'it is going to take me a long time to have a first reading of these. I said first, because if you want me to help there will have to be other readings.'

'I realise that.' She hesitated, then suggested, 'I'm distracting you? You want me to go away, don't you?'

His smile gave assent. She took a last sip of the coffee and stood up, wincing. Now she was feeling the pain of that last hour of tensed muscles and body, but she couldn't bring herself to walk away.

She asked, and couldn't keep the desperation out of her voice, 'You *are* going to read them, aren't you?' She looked away in embarrassment. 'I'm sorry. That was unforgivable, but there's so much of it, and it goes on, and on. That's the really dreadful thing – the way one part led to another that was worse and to another worse still – a kind of terrible avalanche that began with that one small box.'

Slowly she picked up her purse and the white gloves. She was still reluctant to leave them – that stack of white papers that had been part of her for so long, over so many months of patient work.

She told him, 'You've only read Sandra's version so far – '

'From what you say, nothing I've read was later proved a lie?'

'Nothing,' she agreed helplessly. 'Not one word of it, but Peta's story told another all through other eyes.'

Statement of Peta Squire, given to police after the death of Jack Burton:

I first met Sandra Kilby on the morning of 11 January in the washroom of Central Station.

I went to the washroom in deliberate search of someone like Sandra. I mean by that, someone who was alone, and going to be on their own for the first time, because I wanted a roadmate for hitchhiking, and I don't care if it does sound bad but I wanted someone I could boss, or rather, someone who would let me do the leading.

The summer before I made plans in advance and I went away with a girl who wanted everything her way and never mind me, and because she didn't want any help and knew all the ropes as well as I did, we broke up, and I was left on my own. I didn't want that to happen this year.

I knew as soon as I saw Sandra that she needed help. She looked half scared to death and I knew, because it was the way I'd felt my own first year, that she was sure she couldn't go out into the crowd on her own, so I went up to her. I forget now what I said. I just let words spill out, any old thing at all, just so long as she started thinking about something other than her nerves, and it worked, because she started to thaw.

I helped her find a seat on the train and we went on talking. Like I suspected she was new to walking. She had never thought of anything to make her stand out in a crowd of other hitch-hikers, but I didn't force myself on her. I left it to her. She could come with me or not, and she chose to come.

Everything was wonderful till that first night. I'd made myself a clown costume in secret, and the drivers thought it a riot. So did Sandra. At first she did look as though she'd drop dead at the idea of being with me, but once she saw how it got the drivers to stop she changed round and even wanted to wear it herself.

I said no. Because she might have decided she'd do fine alone, with that costume to wear, and she'd simply vanish and leave me flat. I said no, that first night, after I found out she had her own ideas about handing people a straight deal.

It was Sandra Kilby who took that car mascot and everything else.

I was too busy watching the cars come into the service station and summing them up and their drivers, to keep an eye on her. Or to steal anything, either.

I was ashamed that night, and furious with her, too, because she might have spoilt things for everyone who came after us. If someone there in the petrol service station had seen her, or had guessed who took that mascot – well, do you think hitchers would be welcome to hang round there any more?

The men would boot them out. So she could have spoiled things for everyone. I explained all that to her. I also told her a lot of other things. I put the theft down at first to her having soaked up a lot of fool stories about hitching. I asked if she'd heard a lot of rot about souvenir-hunting of this sort being just a lark. I told her it wasn't, that it just gave us all a bad name and it was plain stupid as well as being dishonest. I told her over and over that one of us who did something like that spoiled hitch-hiking for everyone else, and I kept telling her how maybe she'd fixed it so that any hitcher going near that service station from then on would be kicked straight out.

I told her a whole lot and we had an argument. It wasn't a quarrel. Just an argument. The sort of spat you can have and still be friends.

We were friendly when we set out next morning. We were still friends that night. I never knew she took an ashtray from Shell's Inn. If she did, I never saw it happen, and she never told me. She seemed quite happy, and she tickled me. I'd tell her things like no, don't take this car, and I'd say why, and she'd be still as a judge listening, and out would come a little notebook and pencil, and she'd jot it all down. She said something about that going to be her road bible for hitch-hiking in the future. That was why I dubbed her Saint Kilby. It was just a silly joke, because of the way she was always opening her road bible, as she called it.

On 13 January it was raining. Buckets of it. I wouldn't have minded walking in it, but there was Sandra. She was grizzling before we were half a mile out of the hostel, and the grizzles changed to whines, and out and out complaints, and I could see I was about to have a real problem on my hands, so I went into that other service station and changed into my clown get-up and I asked the men if they'd get us a lift.

Sandra cheered up just as soon as we were out of the rain, and she was quite happy again when we got out of the car with that old couple. I didn't pay much attention to her at first. She was always very quiet and never joined in much. That suited me. I like talking.

I was talking when I saw her. I saw her *do* it that time. There was a basket on the seat between us with a whole pile of things in it and a woman's purse on top. The purse was open. I noticed that when we stepped in, but it didn't seem important till I saw Sandra's hand. I was talking, and for some reason I looked sideways and I saw her.

She knew I'd seen. She just looked at me with a sort of, 'Well, who cares?' look to her. I think she was amused. She wasn't a bit scared. She knew, of course, that I wasn't going to start yelling about what she was doing. I just had to sit there and take it. I was so furious I couldn't face her in the street when the old people dropped us. I dived into the café and went straight through to the washroom. I was going to stick my face in cold water till my temper had cooled a bit and I could look at her without letting fly.

Afterwards I told her what I thought of her, and I demanded she show me what she'd taken. She held out that pill box, and I grabbed it off her. I told her she was nothing but a thief.

She said I must be crazy. She said all the girls at her school thought souveniring was fun, or maybe it was only *some* of the girls. I can't remember exactly, but there were other girls who'd been hitch-hiking in previous summers, and they'd come back with souvenirs – things they'd taken – and had shown them round the school.

Sandra had never been allowed to go hitch-hiking before. I think she felt a bit out of things. Her people hadn't so much as let her go to a real ball. The others were ahead of her in lots of things, from what she said, and somewhere or other, in all the talk, there was a dare or a bet, or a suggestion.

Whatever it was finished with Sandra vowing she'd talk her parents into letting her go off on her own, hostelling. She knew her mother would refuse to let her go hitch-hiking. She told them at home she'd go by coach. She told me there in the café that it was all my fault she had gone hitch-hiking, because I'd insisted on it and she'd been scared to start off by herself, but as she was hitch-hiking she bent to souveniring too, to put the other girls' noses out of joint.

I told her to bloody well take the blame for her own actions and that I hadn't pressured her into anything, and just because she was hitch-hiking it didn't mean souveniring, too, but she reckoned that the other girls would call her a fool and 'chicken' if she went hitch-hiking but never came back with a single souvenir of her rides.

I was fed up. I went off to get some coffee. We had it and when she asked me to give her back the pillbox I threw it at her across the table. I didn't want it, and nothing I said to her made much impression. I was sick of her.

I was glad of the rain that night. It meant the hostel was nearly empty and everyone was cold and wet and miserable, so there was no need to try and talk and everything sociable and make out Sandra and I were still friends. We weren't. I told her that night I was going to leave her flat. She didn't seem to care. She just calmly opened that blessed road bible of hers and asked if I had any other tips to pass on. She coolly told me that she thought she'd do fine on her own from then on.

I was so wild I couldn't sleep. I got up real early, and there was no one about, so I sneaked down for a look at the morning paper, and there was the news hitting me that the police wanted us.

I got Sandra awake and outside. She was scared stiff. So scared I knew I couldn't just leave her. She'd likely do something silly, the state she was in. She kept asking me what the police might do to her. I thought the best thing was make her eat something, and I led her to the café.

I couldn't act normally though and when one of the men offered me the paper I snapped at him. I was scared to take it because he was sure to comment on that bit about the wanted girls and Mrs Bossley and everything, and I thought Sandra might have hysterics and give us away.

When we went out I told her I'd see she got a hitch to a railway line or coach, where she could start heading back home. That seemed the best thing for her, but she kept arguing she couldn't make it on her own and that I had to stay with her.

I was fed up, but I got us another hitch. I made sure the car didn't have a radio so there couldn't be a news bulletin and the driver wouldn't start trying to discuss the wanted girls with us.

I didn't remove my step-father's name from my pack because of the fuss. There wouldn't have been time, even if I'd wanted to. I had to practically dress Sandra because she was in such a state. I'd altered the name the previous night. I'd been trying to think of something to do to keep occupied, and I looked at the pack and thought how the name 'Wincham' needled me, on my pack, and I just got the scissors and a needle and cotton and I altered it.

When the first driver left us that morning, I talked Sandra into agreeing to go home, so I gained us another ride to the first town near a railway. I wanted to make sure she really would go home, so I took her to the park till it was time for a train to leave.

She still had that horrible box. She asked me what she ought to do with it. I said, 'Anything, only don't wave the beastly thing under my nose,' and she threw it away. I saw it go into the water. I simply didn't think another thing about it.

Jefferson Shields sat unmoving, fingertips together under his chin, gaze fixed on the opposite wall where a neat undistinguished landscape in a neat undistinguished frame broke the monotony of the grey wall.

He was reflecting that Marion Burton was not only a painstaking woman, but an intelligent one. There, in his office, she had been too tense for real thought. He wondered, if by now, given time and a chance to relax, she had seen through the facade of his office and known it for what it was – simply a background so ordinary and so common that it held no distractions.

Visitors came to his office and looked round it, and their eyes said, 'This place is ordinary, so is this man,' and they gave neither more thought, so that their minds turned inward again. There was nothing to distract them from that. He could hold them silent, and eventually their faces would reveal their real feeling about what they had told him.

Marion Burton's face had expressed such anxiety it had frightened him. Her face had been only watchful and weary, while he had read Sandra's story of that start of that summer holiday, but it had changed to a painful anxiety and eagerness, when he had turned to Peta Squire's version of what had happened.

Her face had told him that she wanted, desperately, that he should say, 'It was Sandra who lied.' She had told him, and repeated it, twice, that she wanted only the truth; that if it was Peta who had lied she would still be satisfied; that there would still be a marriage; that she and Ward Wincham would simply withdraw from their in-laws.

Her face had told him the words were a lie. He sat on, wondering at the character of Ward Wincham, at the real relationship between him and the woman, and between Ward and his family.

He let his hands fall to the desk, flat on top of the spread-eagled papers, as the door opened.

He said gently, almost apologetically, 'Can you remember yourself at sixteen, Mrs Gold?'

There was a wistfulness in his upraised glance. He had never surprised her by a question yet, however absurd. He was disappointed again. She said. 'Yes,' without any inflexion at all.

'How good were you at telling lies? How good were your friends at it?'

'*Very* good. There's so *much* to lie about at that age. There are boys you intend to meet without your parents knowing, for a start. It's amazing the lies a girl can think up to cover something like that. Then there are lies of prestige, status – that's terribly important to a sixteen-year-old. You lie about the number of dates you have and your boyfriends and your home – a whole string of points connected with your prestige. You're discovering the need for social white lies, too – '

He stopped her by asking, 'But how good is a sixteen-year-old at sticking to the lie over months – even years? If you'd lied and for six months you were questioned by police and others, and thrust into the cold limelight with your whole life an open book, could you have stuck to your lies in those circumstances?' He told her the reason why one girl had lied that summer four years before.

She stood a long time without answering, then shook her head. 'I don't know. Of course that would be a desperate case, but – six months – and all those questions, and all that time she'd feel utterly isolated from everyone. I don't' – she told him consideringly – 'think the question of morality would come into it. It's incredibly easy, at any age for that matter, to rationalise what you're doing and make it acceptable to yourself, if your own safety is at stake, but *isolation*, that's a terrible point to a girl of sixteen.'

'And if she knew she wasn't altogether isolated? If someone else, one person, or two, knew, and would lie with her and support her?'

Her gaze narrowed. She said, 'The parents of course? Oh yes, it might be quite possible then. As I said, the question of morality wouldn't come into it. If you couldn't face up to the questions any more, it would be because of that feeling of isolation. The parents would have to know. Or a sister, a brother – '

Jefferson Shields nodded. That was it, of course, he told himself. That was the agony in Marion Burton's face, and her desperation. She was frightened that Peta Squire had lied; that it wasn't the parent who had lied with her and protected her, but the brother, Ward Wincham.

Ward, she had claimed, had gone away from home when his father had remarried, and he barely knew Peta, but the pain in her expression gave the lie to that. Impatient with the knowledge of that lie, he bent over the desk, picking up the next paper.

Statement of Enid Roshton, given to police at Asherton Community Hospital, 3.30 pm, 14 January:

I don't know a thing about where Maggie got the pills. Just as I said to the doctor, there's no one at all in our household who has to take pills of any sort, let alone for anything serious. All I have in the medicine chest at home is aspirin and stuff for coughs and some liniment my father had last year for his bad leg.

That's the whole lot of drugs at our house.

I let Maggie go down the park this morning with her big cousin.

I've questioned Ronnie what happened and he doesn't know either. He had no right at all to do what he did, which was just leave her with a group of other kids. He said there were a lot of other boys his age – that's thirteen – and they a had a cricket bat and a ball – well, I can understand he wanted to join in, but Maggie was in his charge. I wouldn't ever have let her go down there otherwise.

He picked her up later to come home for lunch, and he said she was acting funny then, so wherever she got it, it was something in the park. Ronnie said she couldn't walk straight, and he just thought she was tired out from running around in the sun, so he gave her a piggy-back home.

That was how he didn't know, till he was back, that she'd blacked out and was seriously ill. He couldn't see her face and he was riding her on his back and she was just sort of flopping there.

Then at home he let her slide down. I'll never forget it. Her face was queer and covered in sweat, with her mouth wide open. I never had a chance to question her, and now the doctors say it's fifty-fifty if we ever take her home again.

All I can tell you is she was there in the park. Ronnie doesn't know the names of the kids she was with, except little Sue Jack and Bronwyn Peirce. She's quite a big girl – about eight. She lives in Amaroo Avenue.

Statement by Bronwyn Jane Peirce, given to Constable Evers, in the presence of her parents, at their home:

I went to the park this morning. The others wouldn't play with me. They said to go play with the babies, so I rounded up a lot. Their names were Sue Jack, a little girl called Maggie, Ross Mayne, Andrea Lee, another girl named Dory – I don't know her first name, and a little boy Sue said was Eddie something.

We went to the little pond and Ross took off his sandals and paddled, and he found a little silver box. It was like a rose. I opened it and there were white tablets inside. I know tablets might make you sick. I told them all so and I hid the box in my pocket, in my jacket, only Ross was wild I took it off him and he pinched it back when I wasn't looking, only he threw the tablets out first. I saw them in the grass. I saw Maggie looking at them, only I never knew she touched them. I told everyone not to touch.

I didn't tell anyone about them being there on the grass. I was wild with Ross. I went away to find him. I didn't see Maggie again. I got the box off Ross and I smacked him good and then I went home.

Statement of Constable Evers:

As instructed I have questioned the children named in the statement given by Bronwyn Peirce. All the children have denied touching the tablets. The parents have co-operated fully in a search of their homes. No tablets have been recovered.

As further instructed, Asherton Park, in the vicinity of the pond described, has been searched. Medical evidence is that these tables dissolve on contact with moisture. There was a sharp shower at approximately four this afternoon. There is no visible evidence of the tablets.

Statement of Dr Malcolm Voral, given to Marion Burton:

Yes, of course I remember that January. It was tragedy piled on tragedy, mixed with farce.

I can remember every last thing about that January afternoon. It had been a blazingly hot day, and for an hour of it I was sweating over that baby, Maggie Roshton. She was a bit over two, then. Now she's six and going to school, but when I rushed to the hospital I was sure she was about to die.

You can never be certain, of course, especially with small children. One minute they're at death's door, and the next – the unbelievable has happened.

I remember coming out of the ward, and the smell of wet gum trees coming through the landing window. I looked out and there the world was – awash again, and suddenly all the heat had gone from the day. It returned later and the sun, too – it was only a shower, but I stood there revelling in the coolness and trying to think if there was anything I'd failed to do that might possibly help Maggie.

I went back to the ward as the rain stopped and later I went to the hospital waiting room. The unbelievable had happened for Maggie. it was close on five o'clock then, and, callous as it might sound, I'd already pushed the drama to the back of my mind and I was regretting my lost Saturday afternoon leisure.

You get the ability to switch your mind that way after a while. You'd not stand up to the job if you couldn't, so I was really thinking of a leisurely drink, dinner, and bridge with my wife and friends, when I was telling the parents that Maggie would be back home in no time.

There was the usual scene – the mother weeping and the father swinging from anxiety and agony to blazing rage, blustering and blasting at me as to what he'd do if he got his hands on the person responsible for leaving those tablets about. It's a stock reaction to the situation and you just let them do what they like till the storm is over.

I was waiting for that when the alert came and I knew there was no chance of bridge and probably not of dinner, either.

There had been a crash on the bridge outside the town. One car – there had been plenty of witnesses to facts, because people were returning home from sporting events out of town – had been coming from town and on the bridge it just swung away, straight into the oncoming cars in the other lane. We sent the ambulance, and started scrubbing up – the first alarm had told us seven seriously injured.

Only four had to be kept in the hospital. That was bad enough. The others were patched up and sent home. Three of the badly injured were in one car – the other had been the driver of the car that had gone wild and done the damage.

A police constable was going through his jacket pockets while I was checking him over. I remember asking, 'Who the devil is he? We might have a botched suicide here. He's heavily drugged anyway,' and the constable referring to the licence folder and answering, 'John Mawson Jack, aged sixty-seven.'

It was an unusual name. For a minute it didn't mean anything more than that, then I remembered Maggie's mother weeping over the baby and telling us about the park and the other children who had been there.

The constable got it at the same moment. He said, and he almost yelled it in fright, 'Is it?'

I couldn't know for sure, without tests, but I told him it was likely that the old chap had had the same tablets as Maggie Roshton.

Statement of Sergeant James Dike, at Moori, given to Marion Burton:

Fate has a strange way of pulling tricks on you. I'd been promoted and placed in charge of the Moori area because I'd asked for a quieter district. I'd been close to one of the main prisons before. There had been three bad breakouts while I was there. I was involved in the hunt for the men each time and was wounded in the last.

I'd been in Moori four weeks, and plummetted straight into the mess those girls left behind them. It was a landslide of trouble, beginning with the shifting of that tiny box of pills from its rightful place, and ending with a crash that shook the whole state.

It's a useless exercise going over and over in your mind and saying if only I'd done this, or if I'd only acted a scrap faster and thoughts like that. It doesn't do a scrap of good.

The press had a field day though. I'd been a sluggard, a laggard, a lazy bum and a few other choice things. If I'd found the girls the landslide of trouble would never had happened, Jack Burton would still be alive, a whole heap of people wouldn't have been hurt, a lot of heartache and headaches would never had happened and one girl wouldn't have lived under the shadow of guilt all these years since.

Oh, yes, it's easy to say that, and actually there was no real delay at all. I took official steps to find them, but it didn't seem *urgent*. All along I had the knowledge that in the end Albert Bossley would stop huffing and puffing and carrying on like a lunatic and agree it was senseless preferring charges against the girls for taking that box.

I was positive of it. I set things in train, but there was no sense of urgency. Not till I had that phone call.

There's another funny thing. I'd met the chap who was in charge at Asherton. We served together for three months. I'd been acting as relief that time and we'd kept in vague touch ever since – you know the sort of thing – a card at Christmas with 'Ann's won a scholarship and the wife's made the local tennis team' scrawled on the bottom, that keeps you abreast of what's happened in the other family without all the bother of writing letters and paying visits.

It was a bit of a shock when I heard his voice on the line and when he said, 'Jim, there's all hell loose here' I thought at once of his family.

It wasn't that of course.

He went on, 'We've found your old chap's cursed pill box, but we haven't the pills, or those girls either. Instead we've five people in hospital, four carried away from it in plaster and bandages to be put to bed at home, and God knows how many pills on the loose all over the town here.'

He went on to tell me about the pill box finding its way into the pond in the local park. He moaned at me over the wire, 'If only the wretched box hadn't been watertight this wouldn't have happened, because the docs say the pills dissolve in moisture.'

He told me about the children finding it and about the two-year-old who'd swallowed one thinking it was a sweet, and I learned about the accident on the bridge.

He told me that the old man driving the wild car had been grandfather to little Sue Jack, a four-year-old who'd been playing there in the park with Maggie. He'd been visiting his son and family that Saturday.

He'd been there in the house when the constable had come round questioning Sue about the pills and searching the house, just in case. He described Sue to me, 'a real little picture postcard angel, with gold-brown curls and blue eyes and dimples. She put her finger in her mouth and told Constable Evers she'd never touched the tablets.'

Of course they didn't take her word for it. Kids scare easy, especially when a policeman in uniform comes round asking what they've been doing. She was scared to tell. Especially as she had disposed of the couple of tablets she'd scrabbled off the grass and bought home with her.

Sometimes I wonder if that family have learned to laugh – really laugh – over it all. It was sheer farce, you know, but it led to so much, right down to Jack Burton dying.

There in the park that one kid, the bigger one, told the little ones to leave the tablets alone. She had the right idea, of course, in trying to scare them off, but she used the wrong words. She told them that if they took them they'd grow another pair of ears.

The tragedy was the old John Mawson Jack had been going deaf as a post. He'd said, only that morning, he'd given anything for a new pair of ears.

I should be able to laugh myself, now, but I still can't.

She took two of the pills home and she put them in the old chap's flask. I don't think she believed he'd honestly grow new ears, but she wanted to see what *should* happen. It's funny, isn't it, terribly funny, but I still can't laugh about it, at all.

Anyway he took a drop for the road, said his goodbyes, got into the car, and had that smash, and when he landed in hospital the doctors saw his name on his licence and that he was drugged and put two and two together.

The answer frightened the lives out of everyone, because when they went back to little Sue Jack and told her she'd been telling whoppers, she informed them a lot of other children had grabbed at the tablets and run away with them. She didn't know their names some had been complete strangers attracted to the sight of the other children scrabbling for something in the grass.

The Asherton police moved fast. They had the news over the radio and flashed on television. They sent out a patrol car with a loudspeaker, into the streets, to give warning there. They did everything possible to warn every parent to look for those cursed tablets and question their children. They got on to the press for emergency reports in the later editions and they rang me and told me.

Why hadn't I found those girls before they'd dropped the pills like a bomb on Asherton? I was going to be asked that question more times than seemed possible. It was useless to answer that I'd been doing my best to trace them and to put a name to them both.

We found the commercial traveller who had picked them up after Albert Bossley. He told us he was certain they had taken his order book. He didn't know why, except that perhaps it had been out of spite. He hadn't wanted to take them and had showed it.

He wasn't able to describe them well. For the simple reason he had been angry at having to take them along, he had tried to ignore them, but the tall one, so he claimed, had a big mole on the centre back of her left hand.

The little one had a long fair plait, tied with red ribbon, and her rucksack was new. The other girl's was old. He was quite certain of those points, and it had seemed to him that the two of them might well have chummed up in some hostel on the way. They certainly hadn't seemed to him like old and close friends.

That, of course, went against what Albert Bossley had told us , so I discounted it and went to interview the men at the service station where the girls had grabbed that disastrous hitch from Albert Bossley.

'Too right, they were in here quite a while.' The young mechanic was impatient to get back to the car held high on the hoist. 'No, of course I'm not a friend of theirs. Look, we get dozens of kids in here of a summer. Have a gander round the place. Everyone working here's young, too. The kids on the hitch know we're not likely to slap them down like other service stations – a lot of the older chaps blast them off the premises.

'You can't blame them really. It's damn unpleasant to have a driver come back at you giving you blazes because of some kid he's picked up on your tarmac who's flipped his wallet.'

He shook his red head decisively. 'We've never had that trouble here. I can sum them up to an inch rule. Sometimes I say no, and I say why. I say to their faces that they need a good wash or ask that they prove they're not broke. If they are, you know it's temptation if there's a wallet or food or something saleable, in a car, and a few of them – only a few, mind – aren't proof against the tempting.'

He shook his head again, 'I summed that pair up. Now you say I was wrong, so I'll give you my summary.

'The tall one was used to hitching. She was business-like, she knew the best way to get a ride – that clown outfit was good. Not stupid like some ideas some have, but really good. Eye-catching, but neat and tidy and nothing offensive about it. She could talk well too, but nothing smutty, though she joked a lot. You'd be surprised at how blue some of the girls are, then they scream murder if a man gets the wrong ideas about them. It'd give you a pain.

'She was right, I tell you, and the little one – I'd summed her up as one of those schools where they're taught pretty manners and every term they have a close-of-term ball that reaches the social pages. She was nice-spoken and quite the lady.' He shrugged. 'You see a whole lot of that type on the road each summer now. They think they're real devils and seeing life in the raw because they're stopping cars for a ride.

'If you ask me there wasn't any real harm in either of them. As to them stealing – I just don't get it. They didn't seem that type at all.'

He hesitated for a long time before he answered the next question, 'Describe them? Well, I have in a way already, haven't I? See, I don't go much for physical looks. You could have a crooked nose and a squint and buck teeth and you might be all right so far as I'm concerned. I'm just looking for signs the kids might be troublemakers.

'One was fair, with a long plait. One was taller and had dark straight hair – oh, down to her shoulders,' he gestured. 'Her name was Peta. No, I don't know what else. I wasn't interested, and I don't have a clue to the name of the other.'

Dike jotted it all down. The file was slowly growing. Now the tall girl with the mole on the back of her left hand had a full name – Peta Winchely – and the small one with the long fair plait tied with red ribbon, was St-Something. Irritably he reflected that the growing file would almost certainly gather dust through the years and be turned up some time in the future to mock at his work.

Softly he cursed both Albert Bossley and the girls. He asked, 'Where did they come from to here anyway?'

The younger man looked surprised. He jerked his thumb over his shoulder, towards the hill behind. 'The hostel up there of course. A long line of them came out into the rain. I was watching them. All the colours in the rainbow, bobbing down the hill in a river of colour through the grey rain – it was quite a sight.'

The hostel matron told him, as the other one had, that they had long ago ceased keeping a visitors' book. She smiled at him tiredly, 'They haven't much originality, poor dears, and the same old names keep cropping up, usually with rude comments underneath about the beds and the facilities. Oh, just fun, you know. They're not bad youngsters at all. Most of them anyway. The summer ones, especially, are letting out bottled-up spirits. Exams are over and decided, and off their minds.

'I don't care how high-spirited they are, providing it doesn't get out of hand, or it isn't malicious. Oh yes, we do have trouble sometimes. You'll always get the type who likes slashing railway carriages and breaking up telephone booths. They pull out the plumbing in hostels. Weird, isn't it? I've never fathomed why. I don't think they know themselves. There's just a need in them to destroy. It's terrible. Pathetic, too.

'The two you mentioned?' She shook her grey head. 'I'm sorry. I don't remember them particularly. That means they didn't bring themselves to my notice. They didn't misbehave and they didn't need first aid and they hadn't forgotten to buy food to cook up. You'll always find a few who've forgotten. Sometimes it genuine, but mostly it's because they've run out of money. I try to make sure they go off next day with someone who has some, so there's no temptation to get into trouble. Most of them have made arrangements to pick up cash at banks on their route, but the banks don't open till ten, and they hate waiting around in a town once they've left the hostel.'

She hesitated when he asked her about souveniring, then she admitted, 'Yes, it does happen. No, there's no particular class or type involved. Frankly, I never ask about it. I don't want to be involved. Well, yes, if you like, I turn a blind eye.' Irritably she added, in the face of his implied criticism, 'I've too much work as it is without bothering about things like that.'

'I've told you I don't remember those girls, but there was one girl here that night who never left town. She slipped on the wet road and broke her ankle. They brought her back here from the hospital. She's here till her parents drive up and collect her. You can talk to her.'

Which was easier said than done, as Dike found, because Mary Oliver had no inclination to talk to him. It took coaxing and arguing and finally curtness before she lifted her gaze from her folded arms and admitted, 'Yes, I talked to them and I remember them, but you're wrong, you know. About her name. Peta's, I mean. It's not Winchely or anything at all like that. Oh yes, I'm positive. I can't remember what it is, but it's nothing at all like Winchely.'

She told him she had never heard the others girl's name, 'But she was frightened of Peta,' she added, and stuck to that. 'She seemed a bit of a baby,' her voice scorned. 'She said she had to do just what Peta wanted, but she was frightened of trying to go on by herself. She said she'd never hitch-hiked before and had kept thinking it was easy, but there seemed to be lots of traps. She told me she wished she had never started it.

The request for the two girls 'who might be of great assistance to police enquiries' to come forward, was broadcast and televised that evening, just after the warning to parents throughout Asherton that a dangerous drug was believed to be in the possession of some of the town's children. The report named the drug and listed it uses and its symptoms and how it had come into the possession of the children.

The smash on the bridge was given full coverage. The television cameras had lingered on the twisted wreckage, blocking the road. There was an interview with the parents of Maggie Roshton, and of Sue Jack.

It was followed by an interview with Albert Bossley.

{10}

MARION

However the television station had reached Albert Bossley so quickly and why, when they realised his condition – his rage and his hysteria and his shock – they went ahead with that dreadful television interview, I can't imagine.

Jack had been out playing tennis. I'd been indoors all that day. I hadn't felt well. I'd cried off tennis and had drooped round the house till he came home. I threw some chops under the griller then, and started preparing salad, while I kept one eye and my ears on the television.

Jack was running the shower. I called him to turn it off because there was something important – a lot of people had been hurt because of some drug being left in the park.

I remember Jack coming out of the bathroom wrapping the towel round his waist, and dripping water all over the floor. I was furious with him. It's a queer thing, but after all these four years that's the thing that I remember best – the feeling of fury and impatience.

I can't remember the wording of the report about the tablets, except vaguely. I don't remember at all seeing the interview with the baby's parents, but I can remember the shot of the crash on the bridge. It looked ghastly and I remember Jack giving a long whistle and saying, 'Anyone who got out of that alive was more than lucky.'

We started talking about it and wondering out loud however the pills had been in the pool in the first place. Jack said it was obvious – someone had the box in their pocket and leaned over the water and out popped the box and possibly they hadn't been able to find it again. It had been a sheer fluke, and a terrible one, that the little boy had stumbled on it.

Then we stopped talking. There was the other announcement. I can't remember the exact words. It was very brief and very official, something about the police being anxious to contact two girls who might be able to help enquiries. It said the girls had been hitchhiking and one was described as tall and dark, and her name was Peta. The younger girl was fair, with a long plait and her surname was believed to start Saint-something.

Something similar to that, anyway. I remember asking what that could be about and Jack asking if I hadn't read the morning paper. He was quite excited. I hadn't read it. I'd been feeling off-colour and I hadn't bothered. He fetched it and showed me the report there about the missing drug and the two girls being wanted.

Jack said something about the pair of them being run out of town on a rail if they were found in Asherton. Then he added, 'Poor kids!' I remember quite clearly agreeing with him about that, and saying they couldn't have guessed how things would turn out.

Then Albert Bossley came on.

There was always that half hour after the news when they interviewed people who'd been in the news that day. It has a different man doing the interview now.

Perhaps once the interview started, everyone was so stunned they just let it go on. Anyway it wasn't stopped. It went on and on and Albert ranted. He raved and he almost choked on his own rage. He let everyone know what he'd like to do with them and accused them of every crime he could think up. He threw all the blame for everything squarely on to them. He accused them of killing that baby and all the people involved in the crash – though no one had died at all.

Finally he worked round to describing them. It was all terribly distorted of course – he made them sound monsters. He didn't use the name Winchley. He did say something about the police telling him he'd been wrong about the name and he said he'd seen a name on her things – duds, as he called them – and then he flayed out at her and claimed that obviously she was using stolen things!

There was hardly a piece of nastiness he didn't impute to them. He claimed Peta tried getting money and food out of him and had flounced out of the car when he wouldn't give the girls a free tea at the end of the ride.

When he had finished flaying Peta he worked around to Sandra. A prissy young miss with butter on her tongue, was his description. It might sound a matter for laughter, at this distance, and without seeing it for herself, but spat out in a vicious scream of blind rage, it was appalling. It couldn't have seemed worse if he had let out a stream of obscenity. He spoke about what he called her mock-innocent grey eyes and the very description managed to sound filthy.

It was appalling.

I remember standing there with Jack, watching and listening, and feeling quite sick. I wondered, too, if those two girls were seeing it and hearing it. I was hoping they hadn't. I was sure, if I had been standing in their shoes then, I would have been terrified out of their wits.

{11}

SANDRA

She couldn't go home. It was the one thing she could think of clearly – that she couldn't go home, now, right away, and face all the questions that would go on and on, probing and demanding, till they found out what had gone wrong with the holiday.

She had walked rapidly, almost running, from the park and from Peta, too, but once away from it, out on the grey road again, her speed slackened, till finally she was still.

There was a handy bus seat. She sat down on it, trying to think what to do next, sure only of one thing, that she couldn't go home and face the questioning. She wouldn't be able, she was sure, to hide the fact that she was upset and frightened and unhappy, and they would question till they found out the reason.

After a little while, a fat woman came and sat down on the seat. The seat wasn't secured properly to the base. Under the woman's weight it tilted and Sandra began to slide towards her companion.

The woman noticed it. She chuckled. 'You'd best put lead in your boots, young lady,' she advised, then demanded, 'Where do you expect the bus to take you? It only runs out to the factory and back to town again. You're not going to the factory, that's sure, as it's Saturday.'

Sandra admitted, 'I wasn't going to take the bus. I just wanted to sit down for a while.'

'Feet hurting?' The woman wriggled her own broad feet for inspection. 'You ought to have mine and you'd want to rest them all right. Where are you making for?'

Sandra shook her head.

'Nowhere in particular?' The woman eyed her shrewdly. 'Just walking, and getting fed up with it? I can see so by your face. I don't know what you kids expect setting off across country on your two feet, and getting dusty and dirty and tired out. In my time we used to go to a nice resort, with a case full of pretty frocks and doll ourselves up and flirt with the boys.' She added, almost defiantly, as though she expected derision, 'We enjoyed ourselves, too, and our feet weren't so worn out from walking that we couldn't dance of a night. What do *you* do at night? I bet it's fall into bed, you're so knocked up. That's not fun at all. Wouldn't you fancy dolling yourself up in a nice dress and having a leisurely lie down before a dinner that's all cooked for you and served up nicely, while you're flirting with the boys at the other tables? Then there's dancing afterwards.' She pressed, 'Wouldn't you like that?'

Sandra said, 'Yes,' and said it so explosively, with such yearning for the holidays of past summers, with the ordered, *safe* days, that the woman turned to openly stare.

Sandra didn't notice. She was thinking of the word safe, and other words like it – like sheltered and secure, and comfort, and finding in them a yearning she had never expected.

Then the woman touched her arm. She said, 'You're not the type for walking, dear, and you've guessed. Why not go down to the Boronia? That's the guest-house right over there on the corner.' A fat hand waved the direction. 'They take commercials and the people who come up for fishing, and it's hardly gay, but it's decent, and there's the local Saturday dance tonight. At the town hall. The couple who own Boronia go every Saturday for the old time dance bit.

They'd take you along for the mere asking and you'd have a lovely time.'

She heaved herself up as the bus approached. 'You try it, dear,' she pressed.

Her fat hand waved and her face beamed down at Sandra as the bus moved off. Sandra was left in a cloud of red-tinged dust. It made her cough and she turned her back to the swirl of it, and because there seemed no better idea she started to walk towards the weatherboard building on the corner.

The people didn't like her. She saw that at once, as soon as the woman behind the small desk lifted her gaze. The woman was tall and thin, and her half-begun smile seemed to contract to sourness. Without taking her gaze from Sandra she called and a man came through the swinging door behind her – a tall, grey-haired man in his shirtsleeves.

The two middle-aged faces gazed blankly at Sandra, unwelcomingly and watchfully. She wanted to turn and run away. Her feet shuffled, beginning to move back towards the door, then she stopped, because there was nowhere else to go and she was tired.

She went up to the desk. She said crudely, angrily, 'You don't make your guests exactly welcome, do you? A woman at the bus stop told me to come here. She said the place and the people were decent.'

The woman stood up. She said, 'We're suspicious of hitch-hikers. I'm sorry if you're offended, but we've had trouble here in the past – damaged rooms and unpaid bills.'

Sandra's anger and defiance were both gone. She said help-lessly, in the face of the implied threat they would turn her out, 'I can pay. I'll pay in advance if you like, but . . . I've never walked before you see, and . . . I'm so *sick* of it!'

They were kind. She found that out. They gave her a small neat room overlooking the back garden, brought her warm milk, advised a shower and a rest in the garden later.

As a deserted kitten sinks into blissful sleepiness on finding kindness and a home, Sandra let herself drift in peace. She wasn't afraid that they would see in her one of the girls the press report had mentioned. She had coiled her fair hair into a knot behind her head, and Peta was no longer there.

Only Peta came back. Sandra was half asleep, fair head tilted back as she gazed at the clouds through the tree tops, seeing they had grown misty-grey edges, wondering if more rain was coming, when footsteps crossed the grass.

Peta's voice demanded, 'Why didn't you go home?'

Sandra opened her eyes. She was frightened, and wasn't sure why, except that Peta's voice was angry and commanding and impatient. When she looked up it was to see that Peta seemed someone different entirely.

The new Peta's dark hair was brushed back and held by ribbon and she was wearing the one dress she had packed for the holiday – an uncrushable knit sheath of brown and cream checks. She looked older and vastly different from the Peta of jeans and shirt, and whole worlds away from the gay clown who had danced through the red dust and lifted her hand in command to passing cars.

Sandra accused, 'You've been spying – following me!'

'I've been watching over you. You're such a little *fool*!' There was exasperation and something near to contempt now in the deep voice. 'I didn't know what you might get up to next. You swore you'd head home. You promised me and yet here you are – I saw you come in here and you didn't come out, so I knew you were staying, and that's mad – why didn't you head for home, as you promised?'

Sandra said, 'I'm tired and I couldn't face all the questions they'd ask, and there was this woman – I sat down at the bus stop . . .'

'I know.'

'If you snooped and spied you'll know we talked and she said to come here and forget about walking – I told her I'd enough of it. She said I could go to the dance at the town hall and flirt with the boys and have what she called real fun.'

'Are you going?'

'No. I'm too tired. I just want to sit here and rest. Tomorrow I'll go – oh, anywhere there's peace and quiet and . . .' her face and quick upward look both said, as plainly as words could have done, 'and where there's no signs of you'.

She added abruptly, 'You shouldn't have come here – you aren't staying?'

Peta's brown hand gestured at the frock. 'What do you think, with me rigged up like this? Oh don't worry, they won't connect us. I bought a suitcase and stuffed all my things into it and turned up with a tale of a sick aunt, and coming up to see her, but not being able to stay in the house with illness and a nurse and all, so I came to the Boronia to stay overnight. It'll seem natural if we talk.'

She added impatiently, 'I can't walk out again . . . now, and I had to come in and see what you were up to.'

They were told there would be a selection of cold cuts laid out in the dining room. They could choose what they liked, they were informed, and do what they liked – everyone else had planned on going to the dance.

The day's events hadn't affected Peta's appetite. She piled a plate high with ham and salad and pickles, topped it with wedges of buttered bread and carried it all into the sitting room. Sandra eyed the piled plate with revulsion, then wondered if Peta was maliciously making as much noise as possible over munching the salad.

She turned up the volume on the television, not looking at the other girl. Not till the announcement came. White-faced then, she turned to Peta. The other girl was staring into space. Slowly she turned and their eyes met. They said nothing at all. Sandra thought that no words in the world would ever sweep away the sheer terror and horror of that unemotional voice telling of the pills and the trail of tragedy they had left.

They kept silent through what followed – the call for the two for them to come forward – and sheer inability to speak kept them silent through all that came next – the spewing forth of a man's bitterness and hatred and violence towards themselves.

It was Peta who turned off the set. Her face was quite blank, but her eyes were too bright, and her deep voice roughened and cracked when she said quite gently, 'It's too late to have hysterics, Saint Kilby.' Her brown hands pressed down on Sandra's shoulders. She said, 'No, don't move. You're going to start running. What good do you think that's going to do us?

'It won't help a single scrap. It'll make things worse, because these people will come back and find you gone and what will they think? That you're the girl with the long fair plait, of course, so they'll ring the police and the police will start running, too, Saint Kilby.

'You won't outdistance them. It's not the slightest good running. You must see that. We might as well stay. If they're suspicious of us they'll ring the police. We won't be any worse off than if we've run, but I don't think they'll dream we're the two. Won't they think that those two girls are miles away? They're sure to, you know, and we don't look a scrap like the two we were. Even if they doubt us – people fight shy of being proved in the wrong. What would they say to us if we weren't the two involved, and they bought the police here?

'But, Saint Kilby, haven't you realised that all of them – every last one here – has gone to the dance? You don't sit and watch television in a dance hall. I don't think any of them will know about this. Perhaps someone might come to the hall with a story about it, but they'll concentrate on the smash and that baby, and that horrible man.

'We have to stay put. It's the only way. The very best thing possible. Then in the morning we'll leave and we'll go home.'

Her voice pressed and cajoled and commanded, and Sandra's shock and fright left her with no strength to fight, even if she had wanted to. She didn't particularly want to. There was relief in being able to let someone else do the planning.

She let herself be led upstairs and she took hot milk and aspirin and went to bed and amazingly she slept, and then it was morning and Peta – that strange Peta with smooth rib-boned hair and a slim sheath of dress hiding her thinness, was urging her down to breakfast.

There was no suspicion. It was incredible, but true. On that Sunday morning everyone was sleeping late except themselves and the middle-aged woman who served them and made out their bill. It was quite obvious to them both that the woman was hardly listening to Peta's smooth talk of the sick aunt, of going to see her again before catching a train home, and of Sandra catching the train, too, to a resort down the line.

Once away from the guest house Sandra turned instinctively towards the railway. Peta's hand stopped her. She said, 'They hadn't opened the papers in there and I didn't want to talk in case there was something – I have to see what they say. We'll get a paper and go somewhere quite away from people, to read it.'

The paper boy wasn't interested in them. He turned away, whistling, as soon as he had the money, but Peta made no attempt to see even the headlines. She drew Sandra away. She said crisply, 'We'll find somewhere quiet. I don't want you having hysterics in public if it's bad news for us again.'

They had to go to the park. They didn't know anywhere else that was secluded, and as Peta said crisply, no one would be searching the park for them. It was the last place in the world they would be expected to go.

In a deserted corner of the park, where another big group of Crepe Myrtles flaunted fiery pink against green, they stood still and opened the paper. There was a lot about Albert Bossley and his disastrous appearance on the television screen, and scenes of the smash on the bridge. There were interviews with parents and town councillors and police, and doctors.

All of it came down to one thing – condemnation and anger and bitterness against the two girls.

Sandra was crying. She felt Peta's hands on her shoulders, shaking her violently, but the tears wouldn't stop. She started to speak through them, to tell Peta that she couldn't bear it, that she was going home and she was going to tell her people and the police and get it all off her mind.

Peta's hands dropped away. She said softly, 'You won't, Saint Kilby. If you ever let on about this I'll throw the whole mess squarely on *you*. Cross my heart and cut your throat on it – '

Sandra's fair head jerked back. Her hand brushed tears from her eyes, and then she shrieked in sheer astonishment and in fright, too, because Peta was holding a knife – a wicked thing with a great blade and an ornate carved handle that glittered in the sunshine.

Peta's expression was as wicked a thing as the knife moving towards Sandra's own throat again. It was instinctive to lunge for Peta's hand and try to snatch at the knife. They wrestled and fought, Sandra crying out in fright, and her voice drowned in Peta's shouted, 'You do and I'll cut your throat!'

The man came from nowhere. That was Sandra's impression. One minute the world was grass and sky and the pink blossom of Crepe Myrtles and the next the man was there, thrusting between them, yelling at them to stop it.

Peta's voice threshed at him, 'Get out of the road!' and her hand thrust at him in violent objection to the interference. Sandra saw him step back, clasping at his chest, and the knife, discoloured now, upraised again in Peta's hand.

She ran, and kept running till there was no one in the world except herself.

PETA

It took me a long time to talk Sandra into a reasonable frame of mind, and even when I left her I had my suspicion that she'd just played butter-wouldn't-melt-in-my-mouth with me and that so soon as my back was turned she'd flick off somewhere and start that souveniring all over again – she was so obsessed with beating the others girls at school that she couldn't think straight, if you ask me, and if she started up again she might get caught, and once she was, well, there would be someone to come forward and say I'd been the one with her.

I wasn't going to be drawn into the mess she'd made, any further, so I followed her, just to see if she'd played straight with me about agreeing to go home. I saw her sit down on a bus seat and I could guess that now I was out of sight she was having second thoughts and deciding she could go on alone.

Next thing a woman came along and took the other side of the seat. I could see them talking and then the bus rolled along and the woman left. Sandra stood in the road a bit, then crossed over, walking slowly past the corner building, then coming back. Then she came back once more, and turned again. She kept that up till I was dizzy.

Finally she opened the gate and went up the path, so I crossed over to have a look. There was a plate that said the place was a boarding house. I could have smacked her.

There was no knowing what she might get up to next. I had the horrid idea she'd try a bit of souveniring in that place and bring the police into it. It seemed to me, from what little I'd learned of her, that she didn't learn from mistakes – she just glossed over them and in next to no time she had kidded herself they had never happened in the first place.

I couldn't leave her alone in there, but the police were looking for two girls together, and it might have raised a few eyebrows if another walker turned up on Sandra's heels. I walked round for a while trying to think what to do, then I saw this church. It was Saturday afternoon, of course, and the shops were shut, but there was this churchground and some sort of a sale on, and the first thing I saw was a suitcase. No one paid me any attention. I bought the case for practically nothing, and I put all my things, including the rucksack, into it, and then I went to the railway and I changed to a dress and slicked back my hair and made up my face. I looked a lot different, I knew. Then I went to the boarding house and spun a tale about having a sick aunt and having come up to see her, and realising I couldn't put up for the night there with everyone in a state, only I didn't want to go back home till after another visit to the old lady in the morning, so I'd been told about the Boronia.

I felt a bit mean because they were so kind, telling me I could have free use of the phone to ring about my auntie, but they were too busy to pay me much attention and they and the other guests were going to some dance that night.

Sandra nearly had a fit when I walked in on her. I knew by her face that she'd been lying there in the garden hatching up some new sort of plans, and she realised I was going to put paid to them. She was furious, but she had to accept it, and we had a sort of armed truce by the time we sat down in the sitting-room in front of the television, with the whole place to ourselves.

I'd known all along that faced with real trouble she'd go to pieces. She had hysterics, and started howling, and even vomiting from the shock of the news and the things that terrible old man said about us.

If there had been anyone in the place everything would have finished there and then, the way she was going on but, as I said, we had the place to ourselves. I finally got her into bed and I sat there in her room all night, scared to leave her. I'd talked sense into her – she had been all set to rush straight out of the place – but I made her see how foolish that would be, but if she'd woken in the night I didn't know what she might have done if she'd panicked all over again.

Next morning I said I'd be going home from my aunt's place, and that I'd told Sandra about a resort and she was going to leave with me and take the same train. The people weren't interested.

I wanted to see the latest press reports, so we bought a paper from a newsboy near the church. I didn't dare open it in public, for fear the news was bad and there was another dose of hysterics from Sandra. I had to find a quiet place where I could cope with any trouble, and all I could think of was the park.

We kept away from the pond. I couldn't have gone there anyway, remembering what had happened. I led Sandra into a corner well away from it and then we opened the paper.

There was nothing new – just a rehash of all the horrible bits of the evening before, but the police wanted us and the children's parents wanted us, and the families of the injured people wanted us, and, so it seemed, every last soul in the state wanted us, and when we were found it looked like a whole pile of trouble was going to hit us.

Of course there were tears and hysterics from Sandra. She kept saying it was Mrs Bossley's fault and that the old lady was responsible for everything for the way she had left that little box in open view, for anyone to take.

That was Sandra all over. Nothing was ever her fault. She'd go to tremendous pains to prove it wasn't. She lost her lunch sandwiches one day. That wasn't her fault. It was mine, so she said, and she proved it, to her own satisfaction anyway. I'd distracted her at the vital moment, just when she was putting the parcel in her pack. I should have known that distracting her might have made her forget the parcel. I should have reminded her –

She'd never really grown up, if you ask me. A little kid won't admit it's in the wrong either, and takes a whole heap of pains to prove that fact, but you grow out of that sort of thing. Sandra hadn't.

I'd found it a bit pathetic up to then – till that Sunday morning in the park. Right then it sickened me. I shut her up and I read all the paper report over again and then I said, 'I'm going to the police. We'll have to, Sandra. With all this fuss they're going to have to keep looking for us till they find us and I don't want them dragging me off like a criminal. The best thing we can do now is go to them and show them we're not monsters as that horrible old man is trying to make out. It was a stupid game you were playing, wanting a lot of silly trifles. We'll tell them about that and the hunt will stop and – oh, we're going to get into frightful trouble and we'll be jawed and my people are never going to trust me again,' that was the thing I hated most, that I was going to never be trusted again. I told her, 'The main point is the hunt will stop and with luck all the fuss will die as quickly as it began. If we try to hide though, the hunt will go on and by the time we're finally caught everyone will be thinking of us as a pair of downright criminals. So we're going to the police.'

I could see quite clearly it was the only thing to do, but Sandra couldn't.

I never knew she had that knife with her. I don't know why she ever brought it, but she was such a greenhorn that perhaps she thought a knife was strictly necessary. I just stared at her when she whipped it out and started waving it around.

Maybe it makes me sound stupid, but I almost laughed. It was so silly and I never thought of her as being dangerous, just stupid. Only she suddenly rushed at me screaming she was going to kill me quiet – that I was going to ruin her – a whole pile of rubbish. I don't think she really knew what she was saying.

I was bigger than she was, and I thought I could get the knife off her easily, but she was a whole sight stronger than I ever imagined, and we were fighting like wild cats, when suddenly there was this man.

He was yelling at us and trying to push us apart, and I was so surprised I let go of Sandra, so that he got between us and separated us, only that didn't please Sandra at all. She was half off her head. She didn't know what she was doing, I'm sure, when she tried to thrust him away, and thrust at him with the hand holding the knife. The next thing he was clutching his chest and doubling up, and she was waving the knife and it was covered in blood.

I started to run. I should have stayed to help him, and stop her – I realise that now, but I panicked. I grabbed my case and

I started running. I didn't know where I was going – I just wanted to get right away from all that blood and frightfulness.

MARION

That last Sunday morning was different from other Sundays only in the fact that there were flaring headlines in the newspapers, and we read them together and discussed the whole sorry situation over and over.

It was still very early. Jack never could stay in bed once the sun was up, and when mother had died, and I had started in housekeeping for us, I had had to get up early, too, or he'd start cooking for himself and turn the kitchen into a messy shambles that I was left to clean up.

It's odd how some things come back with vivid clearness, while others can be barely remembered. I can remember quite clearly that the salt shaker needed refilling and because I couldn't be bothered I put the packet of salt on the table. It made Jack cross. He told me I was a sloppy little beast, and I told him that salt shaker was a pig of a thing to fill and why didn't he try for himself? He did and the salt spilled all over the table. That's supposed to mean coming sorrow. If I had been superstitious it would have worried me, but I'm not and I only laughed and told him he had better take up hitch-hiking and souvenir me a salt shaker off some café table, as I was certain no waitress would bother with a shaker that was hard to fill.

He said he'd go for a walk instead – that my cooking had given him indigestion and he'd walk it off. I asked where he was going, because some of the stores opened on Sunday mornings and if he passed one he could bring back some ice-cream – it was too hot for making puddings.

He was going to the park, he said, and when I told him he was a ghoul, he just laughed. I warned him he might find half the town standing by the pond gawking at it, and surely he hadn't fallen to doing that sort of ridiculous thing, and he laughed again and said that rather he wanted to see just which of our neighbours was the gawk-at-the-site-of-the-dirty-deed type.

At the door he looked back and told me that maybe he'd run into the two girls, too, and I told him not to be mad, as they'd be running as fast and as far away as possible. He said something about it being a fact that the criminal always returns to the scene of the crime and perhaps they might be hanging around biting their nails and wondering what awful situation was going to happen next.

He went off whistling. That was the last I saw of him.

I was cross when time flew by and he didn't come home, because there was the ice-cream – I didn't know if he was going to bring it or not, and if not, I'd have to make a pudding, because he grumbled if there was nothing to follow the meat course on Sunday.

I was looking out the window, to see if he was coming, when the police car came. I was just vaguely surprised when two men stepped out and came up and rang the bell. I did wonder if Jack had been parking in the wrong place again – he had been caught twice recently – and when I answered the door I was telling myself it was pretty cool of them to send two policemen just about that, as though he was a criminal, and on a Sunday morning, too.

They tried to be kind and it must be the most terrible job in the world to have to go and tell unsuspecting people that someone will never come home again, but they went about it so slowly that I was nearly screaming in panic and impatience before they had finished.

The first thing I said was a stunned, 'Oh, but you've the wrong name! It couldn't be Jack. He's been out buying ice-cream!'

Absurd, of course, and they convinced me there was no mistake, but I had to go and identify him. That was dreadful and when they brought me back there was the whole street full of people, even down to the children, out on the footpaths, staring at our house.

That was the way it was for a long time afterwards. No one meant to be unkind, but everything I did, every word I spoke, was carefully noted and stored up for later comment among the neighbours.

At first the police had no idea the girls were involved. They tried to make things easy for me, but they had to ask questions. I was no help. It seemed simply ridiculous anyone could even imagine Jack had enemies. He wasn't the type. He didn't drink too much or get into brawls and make off with other men's wives. They got around to suggesting that, too, but I told them they were crazy. Jack wasn't serious about anything except work and he was wedded to that. There had been no trouble at work, either, and no debts.

The whole thing was senseless. I told them that. I suggested it might be one of those cases where a man is beaten up in a park and robbed.

It wasn't that either, they told me. Jack had had money in his pockets, and a good watch on his wrist. None of his possessions had been touched.

It wasn't till later that they traced the knife and learned it had been in the possession of two girls – one a small blonde with a long plait of hair and the other a tall dark girl named Peta.

12

Statement by Inspector Larry Podmore, given to Marion Burton:

There is one thing that you must realise. Neither of the two girls were what is termed a bad lot. Both of them were perfectly ordinary girls of decent appearance and manner, brought up in ordinary decent homes, with ordinary, decent parents. Nowhere in their backgrounds was a broken home, a drunken parent, criminality, backwardness nor even genius – any of the things that might make for a deviation from the normal pattern of humanity.

It is easy to say that they should never have been hitch-hiking in the first place; that hitch-hiking comes down to a bald truth – the taking by someone of something without payment, and that it can lead to a weakening of moral values and conscience, so that the taking of other things, without payment, is but a step.

I can't go along with that. Hitch-hiking has become an accepted part of modern life, indulged in by all strata of society, and encouraged by myriads of drivers themselves. Like many other accepted facts of modern living, it can be distorted and used to excess and for the wrong purposes. On the other hand, used wisely and well, it *can* enrich experience.

It is a means by which the poor-of-pocket can travel, can learn independence and how to get on with people of all classes and very often – Peta Squire was right there – the hitch-hiker earns his passage as company for the driver, or as a help if the car breaks down. It is when the hiker takes it for granted he or she should be given a lift on demand, given food and sometimes cash into the bargain, and begins to look on the drivers as poor mugs, who deserve to be fleeced, that trouble begins.

From Sandra's story it might appear that her companion on that holiday was growing into a type such as that. Peta's story tells instead of a mature, sensible, and clear-headed girl who saw the necessity of maintaining standards of decency and morality, not only for her own protection and self-respect, but to smooth the way of others following after her.

It is easy to say, too, that parents who have their children's interest at heart would forbid hitch-hiking altogether.

Just how many things can you forbid a teenager in these days of a permissive society, and expect to be obeyed? They see other children their own age, doing things forbidden to themselves – I don't say its right for their own parents to meekly back down, but I would like to see groups of parents in conference together, laying down standards for all children in the group, and sticking to those standards rigidly.

We come back to the blunt fact, too – hitch-hiking is acceptable, and in this context Sandra Kilby had been forbidden to do it and only, so she claims, began because an experienced, independent, and more mature girl took her under her wing and showed her how to go about it properly.

Peta Squire was not left to do as she pleased either. Her mother appears a loving and protective one, who was faced with the fact that her daughter's friends were allowed to go hostelling and hiking. She took the only sensible course. To quell any rebellion she allowed Peta to go one year, in the company of experienced girl hikers. Perhaps she hoped that one experience would cure Peta of wanting any more of it. Peta enjoyed the experience, however, there was no trouble, and Mrs Wincham says that Peta had definitely matured through that holiday, taken the first strides to independence and with them had formed a new pride in herself and her abilities. So next summer she was allowed to go in the company of a girl known to her mother. Unfortunately that girl became too demanding, and Peta sought other company in the hostels on her way. She found it, too.

She returned home even more mature, and proud of her ability to mix and make friends easily and on neither holiday had she ever been in the slightest trouble.

Why should Mrs Wincham have hesitated, when Peta, for a third summer, proposed hitch-hiking, and proposed that she should seek out a friend on the way? She had proved herself capable of finding good enough company, of enjoying herself in a sensible, level-headed fashion and of coping with everything on her way.

Whatever you may think of hitch-hiking yourself, and I go along with the moralists and objectors in stating that I dislike it for girls, for obvious reasons, it has become an accepted part of teenage life and of our modern society.

In their whole action of hitch-hiking that summer they were proving their very ordinariness.

Which of them lied I still do not know but, though I was never able to prove it, I am certain that the one who lied had the backing of at least one parent. A parent fighting for the safety of a child is, believe me, the most ruthless creature on the face of the earth. To them the ordinary standards of decency, morality, truthfulness, can be thrown out of the window and discarded, if it means the safety of their child.

There is another point you must understand. None of these parents were bad people. They were perfectly ordinary people caught up in circumstances that were extraordinary.

You could, in fact, call it a crime of ordinary everyday people, because the man who eventually died was an ordinary, fun-loving, sports-minded young man without an apparent care in the world.

Everyone who was involved was the type of person you might pass anywhere, on a street, in any town of the country.

That was the first stumbling block, because nowhere could I point a finger and say, 'This man might be a possible criminal; this woman is a confirmed liar; this man is ruthless and domineering and cruel; that woman is a poor wife and mother and might lack conscience and a whole pile of ordinary virtues.'

Of neither of the two girls, either, could I say that here was the very type who might have stolen and called it souveniring.

There wasn't even in their backgrounds anything that might have led to that sort of thing. You frequently, too frequently, perhaps, come across the type of adult who thinks nothing of coming home from a trip loaded with hotel ashtrays and teaspoons and bathroom towels. They would be amazed if you called it stealing. To them the hotels expect you to take the stuff and that is why they put names and fancy crests and all the rest on them.

There was nothing of that sort in the girls' backgrounds. I went through both homes. I looked in cupboards and under them and on top of them. In neither home did I ever come across a towel, an ashtray, a teaspoon, or anything else that told its story of having been souvenired.

The girls were in contact with others, though, naturally enough. I couldn't go through the homes of every girl in Sandra's school, for instance, and many of the parents were people who travelled extensively by boat and plane and train; who holiday in hotels and resorts.

It is quite possible that girls conditioned by the sight of adults bringing home an occasional 'souvenir' from trips, would souvenir themselves and that the souvenirs should be displayed in all innocence as trophies, at school. It is quite possible that there was a bet, as Peta Squire claims was the case, and that it was Sandra Kilby who took that box and all the other items.

You try and prove it. I couldn't. By the time we reached those schoolmates of Sandra's, the ranks of parents and teachers and girls had closed tight. Do you imagine that one parent, one girl, would stand out and have the world condemn her? I didn't expect it and it never happened. Even if it had, could I have proved anything from it? Sandra could have stated, yes, a dare was made, but . . . that she never carried it out at all.

It is equally as possible that Peta Squire was the one who stole the box. She was the experienced hitch-hiker, and there are endless stories of hikers who steal anything, everything, small things, big things, anything within reach of their greedy hands.

So – which of them lied?

I never found out.

All along I told myself if I could find just one thing out of those two stories that was a lie, the rest would fall into place, but find it? All

I did was prove it was impossible to find. Only one point showed where I had sudden doubts, where I said to myself, This looks like the truth, and the other story looks like lies. Because it is best another investigator comes to this story with an open mind, unbiased by any comments I make, I shall not mention it here, and the point, in any case, led me nowhere.

We questioned the girls for six months, then we apparently dropped the case and let them think everything was over, then we went back, out of the blue, and began again, but neither of them faltered. Their stories remained as unbreakable as they had in the beginning. We questioned them endlessly and we questioned the parents and their teachers and their neighbours and all the people they met on that summer holiday.

In the end we still faced that question – which of them lied – without an answer.

In the beginning of the investigation into Jack Burton's death we had no idea the girls were involved at all. Certainly he had died in Asherton Park, and Asherton Park happened to be very much in the news that Sunday morning, but that meant nothing, except that when there's news of that type, there is a queer compulsion on the part of various cranks and odd-balls to make for the scene.

We did wonder, once the investigation had begun and it seemed there was no motive for the crime at all, if some mentally ill person, attracted to the park by the publicity, hadn't committed it, but then we traced the knife – or rather, we sent out press publicity, with pictures of the weapon – and asked for anyone who'd sold such a knife – it was unusual, with an elaborately carved handle which had not left fingerprints – to come forward.

Quite a few reports had come in from various stores throughout the state, when we received another. A knife had been – not bought, but *stolen* – from a store, and the owner was sure that the theft had been committed by two girl hitch-hikers and he described them – a short fair one with a long plait and a tall dark one.

It seemed a bit too much altogether. It seemed like someone angling for publicity. We get a lot of that type with every crime that's committed, but it couldn't be ignored.

I wasn't in a good temper at all about it. I ordered the storekeeper brought to me. I wasn't going to waste time going to see him and I was getting ready to blast him straight back out of the office.

I never did. He was quite definite, and though a bit nervous, quite assured – and he knew the name of the fair one.

He told us as soon as the fuss began over the missing pill box he had recognised the descriptions, but he had done nothing. What was the good, was the burden of his cry. He had once handed two hikers over to the police for thieving. It had involved him in months of questioning, statements, court appearances and unpleasant publicity, and in the end the boys had been given a lecture and had gone off smirking.

So he did nothing, just read the papers and kept his mouth shut, until the day the press ran the description and the photo of the knife.

His story was quite clear. It had been the second day of that disastrous holiday for the girls. They had entered his store, a small roadside country one, selling just about everything under the sun. The tall one had wanted postcards and had stood chatting to him while she looked through his stock.

The other girl had wandered away through the store. He had kept one eye on her, but he hadn't seen her take the knife. Nor had he seen the tall one take it. When she had finished with the cards she had wandered away while the fair one bought sweets. That was all he could state definitely. The knife had been to one side of the counter, in an elaborate sheath. The only one in his store.

It had been there before they had entered. It was gone afterwards. In between only two people had entered the store, both well known to him.

The girls had taken it. Which one he didn't know, but the fair one had dropped her rucksack from her back to the floor. His eyesight was good. He had seen the name clearly.

The fair girl's name was S. T. Kilby.

We remembered that the tall one had called her Saint-something, and we counted on it being St Kilby, not the initials S. T. at all, till a boy came forward. On the evening of 11 January, in a hostel, he had talked to a girl who had told her name to him and the name was Sandra Teresa Kilby.

We were led astray again. We jumped at the Teresa, the name of a saint and told ourselves that there was the reason for the name of the saint that the grocer's assistant had heard.

Anyhow with the name Sandra Teresa Kilby in our hands we went through the records of births of girls of fifteen or sixteen years before, looking for that name.

We learned that Sandra Teresa Kilby, sixteen years of age, was the daughter of Glen Howard Kilby and Teresa Ann Kilby, that Glen Kilby at the time of her birth had been an accountant and that they had lived in the city suburb of Daviston.

They had moved only once since then. It was the Wednesday evening after Jack Burton had died that we knocked on Sandra Kilby's door.

By then, of course, days had passed. Whatever had been her physical and mental state on the previous Sunday, she was composed by that Wednesday evening – too composed altogether.

She told her story without quibbling, and she gave us the name Peta Squire, and the name Wincham and the name of the street and the suburb where Peta lived.

When we went there it was the same thing. The girl who met us was composed and calm. As Sandra had admitted doing, Peta had confided in her parents. Each interview had that in common – blank-faced, controlled parents flanking a cold, calm, composed girl who threw all the blame and the guilt squarely on to the other.

As I said, we kept at it for six months. We probed and we sifted and we questioned – endlessly – everyone who had contact with those girls.

13

Miss Isabel Chase was a gentle looking woman with a mind of cold steel. Podmore found that out in the few first minutes of meeting her.

She eyed him levelly, as she might have eyed the girls in her charge. She said without hesitation, 'I don't believe it. There are certain standards we instil in the girls. That we expect them to keep. They know what the result would be if they did not. A private school lives or dies by its reputation, Inspector. We cannot afford – ever – to have a girl who can ruin us by bringing us bad publicity.

'The girls know that stealing is a crime, no matter what variety of stealing it is. One may steal jewels, or money, ideas, or the answers to examination questions, or public property, such as post office pens' – a fleeting grace of humour softened her cold expression – 'though why anyone ever should I cannot fathom, they're such dreadful items.' She shrugged the humour aside.

'The girls are told all those things constitute stealing, along with the taking of plants from wildflower reserves, or flowers from a private garden. Oh, yes, I know what you're about to say.' He was gestured to silence. 'I admit that in their homes many people pay lip-service to all that we tell the girls, but the point is we have more to do with the girls than the parents do. That's the blunt truth.

'I think it is *our* grounding that eventually rubs off on the girls and Sandra is – sixteen, if I remember rightly and has been with us since she was eight. A total of half her lifetime, Inspector.

'I couldn't bring myself to believe that suddenly she turns her back on honesty and stoops to this – and such a petty business! Trifles she could have afforded to buy honestly. I couldn't bring myself to believe it.'

Looking into her eyes he had known that what she really meant was she refused to make herself believe it. She had her mind fixed in that stubborn refusal and nothing he nor anyone else would say would move her a jot.

It was a relief to them both when he left the subject, asking her to tell what she really thought of Sandra.

Her voice had grown less cold by the time she had spoken a few words.

'Sandra is rather childish for her age. She is an only child, of course, and we endeavour here to see such children visit as much as possible to the homes of other girls – to see family life in the round as one might say.

'Sandra is quite popular. I have never known her to have a serious falling-out with any other girl. We keep a check on that sort of thing, because if it isn't cleared up there's a tendency to have the girls take sides and it ends with one group of girls barely speaking to another.

'On the other hand she doesn't join in group activities to any great extent. We have various social events at weekends through the school year. Sandra rarely attends them.

'Some of the girls don't.' She hesitated. 'Some parents don't encourage it because of the expense. They see that the girls go to the more ordinary events, but that's all.

'It's a sacrifice for a lot of parents to send the girls here. I know quite well what's said about this type of private school – that it's merely a marriage market – that the parents scrape to send them here so that the girls will meet the brothers of the richer girls.' Quite frankly she added, 'In a way it's quite correct. It's perfectly natural that parents want the best marriage possible for their girls, but we never accept a girl here who might have real trouble in keeping up the standards set by the others, from the financial point of view.

'Sandra's parents are quite comfortably off, and she is an only child. Whether they decided expenses should be limited throughout her schooling, or until her last years here, I couldn't say. I would rather believe that her mother is simply over-protective. Sandra is her baby.' She pursed her lips in disapproval. 'She dislikes the idea of losing the baby to the grown woman.'

After a brief hesitation she added, 'Her father is inclined to indulge Sandra in whatever she wants. It is the mother who says no.

'As I said, so far she hasn't joined in much social activity, but it is when the girls are in their last years here that they actually begin a full social life. I have been hoping that this year would see Sandra blossoming.'

Her glance slid away. He could see her white teeth biting into her lower lip. He wondered what Sandra's prospects were of ever coming back to the school and he put the question bluntly.

She didn't like it and tried to evade it with, 'Perhaps her parents would prefer to keep her at home till this unpleasantness has ceased to be public.'

'What you really mean is, until she is proved to be innocent? Don't you?' He flung this comment at her. When she didn't answer, he added, 'You've told me you're sure Sandra could never have begun that souveniring or killed Jack Burton. Yet you won't have her back. Can't you see that one statement cancels out another?'

There was both anger and impatience in his voice, because he had hoped from her something that might lead him to a decision as to whether Sandra had lied or not.

She said helplessly, 'But Inspector – you see – I can't credit it, but how can one be absolutely sure?'

'How can anyone be sure?' The words echoed in the still hot air. 'You can say for yourself that such and such could or couldn't happen, but there's human nature, human panic. You just can't know how people, even people you imagine you know well, would react to this factor, or that, or another. Now can you?'

Hubert Treasland was totally different from Isabel Chase. He was a short, stout, bouncy little man with a good humoured expression and a furrow of concentration lines across his broad forehead.

He stood by the window of his office, looking out over the huddle of buildings, new and old mismatching in a tangle that was neither beautiful nor convenient.

It was a far bigger school than the one Podmore had just left, and it sheltered far more children and it was co-educational.

Those factors made a big difference. Hubert Treasland said so bluntly. His voice was good and pleasantly accented and quite assure, when he said, 'Peta *fits* in here. You could say in another school – the type of place that other girl attends – that a girl was popular and was never in trouble, and that would be all. There's a vast difference here. For a start, there are more children, and the more you have the wider variety of types. For another, this is a state school. The children come from all kinds of homes – from the very poorest to the quite well-off. Thirdly, the boys and girls are mixed together.

'You take a school such as the other girl attended, and you'll find it fairly easy for a girl to get on well with other scholars. She has a head start at it from the word go, you might say, because all the children have an approximately comparable home life, they are all girls and because their parents move in much the same limited circles, both in the business world and in social life, so that the girls are conditioned from birth towards one type. I mean by that they are all well mannered, all attend classes for dancing and tennis, and so forth, all go to the same group of children's parties, all are limited to seeing one small corner of life.

'Here it's a different matter. I don't think that any child here is actively unhappy, but they're thrown in with a vast number from a different social and home life strata altogether and forced to find their own feet, friends to their own taste, and to ward off, without indulging in open warfare, the ones not to their taste.

'Some never make it. They go through life in school dodging blows on the one hand and making life hell for others on the other, forming just a few friendships and shutting the rest of their classmates out altogether.

'Some of the girls can't manage the boys and vice versa. Some girls are frightened or angered or disgusted by the boy's awkwardness and teasing and blundering, while some boys are terrified of the girls, and the girls know it and pick on them.

'The point I am trying to make is that a child who fits into every niche where you can place it is someone who has learned to stand firmly on their own feet, has self-assurance, without brashness or being overbearing and has a very good ability to get on with all types of people.

'Peta *fits*. She has a wide circle of friends without being very close to anyone, she gets on well with both boys and girls, her work is good without being outstanding, and I have never known her to show a grudge, a maliciousness, towards another child.

'As for souveniring – ' He grimaced, turning from the window to come back to the desk. He shook his head. 'Oh yes, it's common. Every time there's a sports meeting or dance, there's always some silly fool who souvenirs the flags or the starter's whistle or some item belonging to the bank, but I'd say it was due more to showing off than anything.'

His shrewd glance met the other man's for a long moment. He said quietly, 'The ones you least expect are often the ones who do it. It's often the shyest, the most withdrawn who owns up to it in the end. They're the ones who're dared to do it by the more extrovert children. If they don't they're "chicken".' He suddenly grinned. 'Ever been dared to shin up the school flagpole when you were a lad? It was a matter of honour to do it and prove you weren't a coward, wasn't it?' What I'm talking about comes down to the same thing.'

Podmore said sharply, 'But Peta isn't the shy, introverted type. You're throwing the ball squarely into Sandra Kilby's corner, aren't you?'

'I'm trying to show you that you can't possibly say that there is any type of child who won't souvenir. There are too many reasons why they might. There's greed for the item concerned, there's the sort of senseless gathering of trifles such as taking hotel ashtrays, there's the question of honour about performing a dare – a whole host of reasons.

'All I can say it that it doesn't seem likely to me that Peta Squire is the culprit. She has hitch-hiked before – no, I don't say I approve of it, but it seems to be accepted conduct every-where – and she has never been in trouble of any sort about it, and I'd say she had too much maturity, too much self-assur-ance, too much plain commonsense to accept a dare. Dared to shin up the flag-pole, I'd say she'd tell the other concerned to shin up himself as she had better things to do!

'She has grown up very quickly – too quickly perhaps – in this last year. Her form mistress has talked to me about it. Peta's mother remarried. Her father had been dead just a year – he died two years ago. It's not easy to lose one parent and be given a new one in a matter of twelve months. The Winchams are fine people, and Peta has no grudge against Mr Wincham. I've made sure of that as if there had been anything like it we might have been able to help her with counselling, and so forth. The trouble is he is a very reserved man and he didn't know what to do with well – ' He smiled. 'Call it an instant daughter!

'Peta made a very revealing remark about the situation to her form mistress. She said, "It seems at home as though we have guests every night for dinner." It brings the situation vividly into life, don't you think, Inspector? Party manners all round and everyone on their best behaviour while wish-ing the evening was over and they could kick off their shoes and relax.

'Mrs Wincham has naturally new things to think about, and I should say Peta has been thrown very much on to her own resources. In other words, she has learned to be self-sufficient, and is mature, and self-assured.

'No, Inspector,' he shook his head, 'I can't see Peta in the role of villain in this unpleasant business.'

Podmore demanded bluntly, 'Are you having her back here in the school?'

The man became still, his face quite blank. he said evenly, 'A state school principal has to accept any child who asks for enrolment, you know.'

Podmore stood up. He said, 'I didn't, and it hardly answers my question. Would you yourself willingly take her back?'

There was only the evasive, 'I think that, until everything is forgotten, her parents might prefer to keep her at home.'

It was desperation that brought Podmore to thrust aside the carefully compiled reports that had flowed into his office from police of surrounding districts, as they had followed the girls' trail from home to its disastrous ending in Asherton Park, and contacted witnesses who had come into contact with the two girls along the route.

He decided on seeing them himself. Somewhere, he was sure, there had to be someone who could pinpoint some small item, some small tell-tale movement, and cry, '*She* was the one who stole; she was the one who had the knife' and lead the police to the point where they could say with certainty, '*She* is the one who lied.'

The waitress who had served them and the two women who had treated them to tea, in the Shell Inn, remembered the party well, but only because they had all appeared so relaxed, so happy and because Peta had been a clown.

'You might've thought they were a family group, only getting on better than most families that drive in here,' she told him cynically, standing sway-backed, feet planted apart, and her arms crossed over her flat chest, as she talked.

'Some of them are at such cross-purposes when they land in here it's like a battlefield all the time they're eating. They're arguing about routes and maps and wrong roads till your head spins listening to them.'

Oh, certainly, she admitted cheerfully, grinning a gold-filled toothy grin at him with no trace of embarrassment, she had listened to that particular party. She always listened. It made the job worthwhile and some of the talk was fascinating.

'Not them, though,' she denied. 'They were just happy. The two women were letting the girls do the talking – or rather, the tall girl was doing most of it. I stopped them, you know, when they came in, because fancy dress seemed a bit much, but there was only this one of them togged up and the old ladies got annoyed, so I let them in. They didn't look as though they'd cause trouble. That's why the boss has the rule, no fancydress – we had some characters in here togged up in all sorts of fancy gear, and there's usually trouble with them.

'Not this lot, though. The tall girl was talking about places she'd seen on her other holidays. No, I can't remember the fair one doing much chattering, but she seemed happy enough.'

She hadn't seen the ashtray go either, but when they had left she had noticed its disappearance. She shrugged it off with a quick, 'Well, it takes all sorts, doesn't it now? You'd be surprised the ones who slip them into their purses. When I started here, we had chrome ashtrays. Shaped like shells like these plastic jobs we have now. They cost a bit, and the boss didn't like it when they started growing legs and leaving home' – the gold-toothed smile flashed again – 'so he had these plastic jobs made. We've boxes of them out the back.

'It doesn't matter much if they go. They didn't cost any-thing much and the boss says it's like advertising – his name's on them, and people who see them will remember the name maybe and call in to get a shell for themselves, but the main thing is they'll eat here, too. So he just slapped a few pennies on the prices of everything on the menu and put the whole thing down to advertising.

'I didn't think much about the ashtray going from the table. I just got another from stock.'

She could tell him nothing else. She grew impatient in the end. She threw at him, 'You seem to be trying to get me to make things up. Is that going to help you?'

The two women who had treated the girls to tea were cousins – Miss Ann and Miss Joan Vockler. He interviewed them in the small home unit they shared above the city harbour. They were quiet, reserved and finicky in their dislike of the whole subject.

They resented his coming bitterly, and they loaded their reluctant answers with so many amendments and alterations that at last he lost patience with them.

Tearfully, Miss Ann saw him off. Her voice floated after him down the stairs in sad bewilderment, 'They were such *ordinary* girls.'

Podmore was beginning to dread the word. It cropped up again when he interviewed the woman who had driven them from close to the truckies' café, to the turn-off to her brother's farm.

She told him bluntly, 'They seemed such an ordinary pair of schoolgirls on holiday that the rest of it is impossible to swallow. Oh yes, when I picked them up that morning I saw that one had long fair hair – not in a plait, of course – and I'd read about the two who'd stolen the box of pills. I did wonder if they might possibly be the two, so I looked at their packs – Detective Dora that was me,' she mocked at herself, 'and neither name was Winchely.'

'They seemed quiet. The older looking one claimed to have a headache.

'No, they didn't talk to one another. I left them by the side of the road, near the turn-off to the farm. They seemed to me two very ordinary girls.'

The words echoed again in Podmore's ears when he caught up with the driver who had taken them on that last hitched ride to Asherton.

'They were ordinary as lambs in springtime.' The man was

small and middle-aged and wizened more than his years justified. He had been driving a small green panel van, and he said roundly, 'Look chum – Inspector, I mean – I had twenty-two flaming payments left on that van. D'you reckon I was going to pick up anything *bar* ordinary looking kids? You pick up something extraordinary and you're likely to find yourself and your van in trouble.

'They were three miles or so out of Asherton when I saw them, holding a lot of fruit and half spilling it and like I said, they were as ordinary as lambs in springtime. I opened the off-side door and in they got and the bigger one said, "Could you take us somewhere near a coach or train line?"

'I said to myself that here was two'd found hitch-hiking a mug's game and were settling for something a bit better, so I said to them that Asherton ought to do them, as the coaches came through, and the trains, too, and Asherton was where I left them, and why didn't I come forward straight away when the row started? Look chum – Inspector, I mean – I *live* in Asherton. D'you reckon I was going to be popular when it came out I'd brought them and dumped them and their pills and trouble into the town's lap?

'Of course I had to come forward after that chap was dead and you fellows got the knife pointing straight to the girls, and what d'you reckon my life's like now?' His eyes were filled with bitterness. 'Half the neighbours won't speak to me, that's what. Too right it's unjust, but that's human nature, mate – they want a scapegoat and I'm it, but believe me, if you'd asked could that pair stick a knife in someone I'd have laughed.

'They were ordinary as a couple of lambs in spring.'

That haunting word echoed again round the hot stretch of asphalt in front of the service station where the two girls had hitched their first ride of the trip.

The man was older than the one who had gained them the ride with the Bossley pair. He was slower of speech and thought and slower to pronounce judgment about them. He weighed thought carefully, one hand brushing slowly over his right temple where the dark hair was silvering.

'I wouldn't say I noticed them particularly at all. Anything else would be telling you a lie. It's easy to claim hindsight and say you noticed this or that that pointed to possible trouble, but it's not true. They must have gained a hitch immediately the girl changed into that costume of hers, because I didn't see it at all. When I saw them they were both wearing jeans, and I remember them only because they took two bottles of coke from that machine' – he gestured to the far side of the asphalt apron – 'and they carefully put the caps into the rubbish can. It gets on my nerves.' He smiled apologetically. 'I watch people go to it, and I wait for them to flick the caps on the apron. Most do. I have to go down and pick them up, else the first car pulling in towards the machine for coke grinds them into the asphalt. In hot weather it's likely to soften so that the caps grind right in.

'The girls put the caps in the rubbish can. Would you call kids like that trouble makers? I don't like kids hanging round here for hitches. If there's ever a complaint I get the backwash, but I turned a blind eye to those two. If they were so particular about the caps they wouldn't be likely to have someone complain about them. Wouldn't you have said so yourself?'

He denied absolutely having even known the little chrome mascot had been taken from the van that had called in.

'The traveller can't have known either till he was gone from here, or he would have said. I saw him off,' he explained. He hadn't seen the girls at all then, and he had promptly forgotten all about them.

'They were just two ordinary kids. Tidier than most. That's all.'

Podmore went back to his office. The long journey had gained nothing. If everyone was to be believed two ordinary schoolgirls had gone on vacation and stepped right out of their ordinary manner of living and standards.

14

Letter sent to Marion Burton four years after the death of Jack Burton:

Dear Miss Burton

I am writing to you against my own wishes, simply because Inspector Larry Podmore has contacted me and asked me to co-operate. I owe him what I consider a debt for the humanity with which he treated all of us during the enquiries. It was a humanity both unexpected – because I was conditioned by unpleasant press publicity to think rather hardly of the police – and deeply appreciated.

That is why I am writing you, but I must say first and say it forcibly – it would be intolerable if the case is raked over again and all of us forced back into the blaze of publicity. Inspector Podmore, in his letter to me, has explained your motives. I appreciate them, but I repeat, any further publicity would be intolerable. This letter, I hope, will answer your enquiries and allow you to see for yourself that wherever the blame lay, it was not on Sandra, and she has a right to the measure of peace that she has gained in the years since that dreadful summer.

You perhaps know that my marriage unfortunately has come to an end, but Glenn still sees all he can of Sandra, and in this respect she still has both parents. Only our home address has changed, and the fact that Glenn no longer comes here except to visit.

She has accepted that situation as it has not meant her losing Glenn altogether, and she has accepted the fact that it seems impossible she will ever be cleared of the blame for the events of that summer. If you had new evidence that might possibly clear her, I would be the first to ask you to have the case re-opened, but please bear in mind that four years ago enough lies were told to condemn Sandra to disgrace. Can you honestly believe that now those lies will be taken back?

One of the hardest things for her to accept was that her school life was over. Perhaps you did not know that? She was by no means a brilliant student – even I must admit she was quite ordinary – but she enjoyed school, and she was looking forward to an extended social life. I had always felt she was too young, even for her age, to join in the more sophisticated events at school. I was waiting for her sixteenth birthday and her senior years at school.

She never had those years. When I tried to take her back I was told it might be better to keep her at home – for a while. It was obvious everyone thought I was remarkably tactless in having tried to re-enroll her in the first place.

So – she didn't go back. She missed those senior years and its social life. She missed her old friends, too. Suddenly, so it seemed to us, doors were closed to us. Of course no one said outright why. Various excuses tried to soften the blow. It was pointed out that she was no longer a member of her old school; she could no longer take part in social events connected with it and most of the other girls' social life revolved round it.

We had her tutored privately. That was easy to arrange, but it was no substitute. She had lost the company of other girls. Even though her pass in the final exams was quite good, she had no wish to go on to university. She would have met there the girls from her old school, you see. It would have been inevitable that whispers would have begun and circulated and she would be shunned again.

My marriage was being dissolved by that time. I deliberately reverted to my maiden name of Smith – such a nice, safe name! – as Sandra was going to live with me. She took it also, so now she is Sandra Smith. She took a business course and she is working as a secretary-receptionist in a small hotel. She enjoys it very much and is meeting people and not leading a life confined to a small office and myself.

She is, you see, beginning to lead a normal life again. For a long time she dreaded meeting people. I couldn't have her revert to that state again.

As to the events of that summer – you must have read the newspaper reports and statements, but of course you cannot read in them the shock and despair of her home-coming that January.

I didn't want her to go on that holiday in the first place. Always before, Glenn and I had taken her to some resort, where we stayed at a decent hotel and where she had holiday companions of a certain standard. I have always been particularly careful that she made worthwhile friends. That was one argument against this holiday in my opinion. I told Glenn she might meet with heaven knows what types.

It was exactly for that reason that Glenn wanted her to go. He was impatient with me. He told me, 'For heaven's sake, Tess, you wrap her up like a baby! She's sixteen and sooner or later she's going out into the world to get some sort of a job and mix in the rough and tumble of business and social life. The sooner she learns how to handle and be friends with all types of people, the better for her and the easier for her once she's left school.'

With both Glenn and Sandra against me I was forced to give in.

I did, however, put my views very plainly and forcibly when the question of hitch-hiking was raised. I wouldn't agree to that under any circumstances, and Glenn kept quiet when he saw I meant it, so that was that – or I thought it was – but I am certain Sandra would never have disobeyed me but the fact the other girl was so capable, so self-assured, and put so much pressure on Sandra. I think she did it so she could prove to me I had been wrong about hitch-hiking.

I didn't dream she would disobey, but it's a fact that she did, but don't take that as a sign that she was – well, underhand. She was not. I have said she was young for her age then. She allowed herself to be taken over by bossy girls and bossed by them. Sandra herself told us afterwards that the other girl talked and talked and laughed at her and called her a baby for being frightened to hitch-hike. She didn't like that at all.

It makes Sandra seem weak-willed perhaps. She was not in reality, but she was shy and because of that she didn't like trying to stand up for herself and getting into arguments and – an important fact I think – she was alone in a world that was totally new to her. She must have felt lost and very alone. I have read that other girl's statement. She says herself how lost and frightened Sandra seemed when she first set eyes on her.

Sandra was ripe for being bossed. She wanted someone to take the lead and look after her, and there was no one who stepped forward to do it except this other girl and Sandra discovered that it meant hitch-hiking with her, or being left alone again.

I can understand how very easy it was for her to go with that girl.

I know nothing of any bet, any dare, any talk among Sandra's friends of 'souveniring'. It sounds ridiculous. In our home such behaviour would be called by its proper name – theft.

Certainly we read that small item in the press that Saturday, about a pill box being stolen and we noted that one girl had a long fair plait, but can you remember that summer? Long hair was in fashion and every girl on holiday, it seemed to me, had plaited her hair.

It meant nothing to us, because Sandra wasn't hitch-hiking in any case. We simply sat back, waiting for the first letter or postcard to tell us how she was enjoying the experience of living in hostels.

Even that evening held no meaning for us. Why should it have done? We were horrified about events of course, but Sandra's name wasn't Saint-something and she wasn't hitch-hiking and Sandra was not a thief. How could we possible connect the two girls? Could you imagine any parent listening to such things and immediately deciding their daughter had changed so much she was the one involved? It would be ridiculous.

Sandra came home late the following evening.

There had been no word from her, and I was actually thinking of her and looking forward to the next morning, because it would be Monday and the mail would probably bring a letter or card from her. Then I heard the door open. I didn't think anything of it because Glenn had gone out and hadn't returned and I thought it was he coming in, but when I said his name nobody answered. I went into the hall. Sandra was standing there.

The whole look of her told me something was terribly wrong. It wasn't just her unexpected return. It's difficult to explain, but her face seemed a doll-face. All life and expression had gone from it.

Strangely enough, when she spoke her voice was quite normal. She said, 'I've come home, mother.'

I remember asking, in astonishment, 'But why?' and I was feeling dreadfully frightened, because of that doll-look to her face. You're a woman yourself. Perhaps you'll understand that I was thinking she'd been attacked. It's the first thing a woman thinks of, I expect.

Then she said, 'There was a man', and I remember thinking in agony that Glenn wasn't home, as though Glenn being there would have immediately put things right.

When she added, 'He's dead,' I simply knew bewilderment. I led her into the sitting-room and fetched brandy and rubbed her hands – they were burning hot, not cold as I'd expected – and finally I made her talk. We were still in the middle of it when Glenn came in and that meant starting everything over again.

There was no hesitation, no signs of her lying. She wasn't hysterical or confused. Just terribly, terribly shocked. Her story was perfectly clear and sensible. It was the story she later told to the police, and the story she has kept to all these years since, and for all the millions of words the police have taken down in evidence, she is still in the position where no one can say she is innocent or guilty.

If you have new evidence, tell the police, but you haven't told it to Inspector Podmore, or he would never have written to me without telling me. That means there is none.

We have suffered enough from it all. I know you have suffered, too, and I am sorry which, of course, is a pathetic commentary on something so terrible. For your brother to die that way, so senselessly, just because he tried to help, is something unbearable to me as it must be to you, but we have suffered for it all the time since.

I can only ask you to let us keep what peace we have made for ourselves.

Yours very sincerely, Teresa Smith

Statement of Ward Wincham, given to Marion Burton:

It's said that if you keep a thing for seven years, you'll find a use for it. Well, my father loved Peta's mother for seven years and in the end he was able to marry her. Which sounds as though the pair of them were meeting long before the marriage, behind Squire's back. That is far from the truth. Whatever my father might have wanted and might have urged, for all I know, Peta's mother is not that type, and she was – I am quite certain of this – exceptionally fond of her first husband, even if not madly in love with him.

My father was a frequent visitor to the Squire house for a couple of years before Peta's father died, which makes it even stranger that I never met Peta till after the wedding.

Several times I was supposed to go to the Squire house. I can't remember now what happened each time but, whatever occurred, I never turned up. Of course, by the time my father was first meeting the Squires I was grown up, or I thought I was. I'm speaking now of twelve years ago. I was eighteen. I had my own affairs and interests. I wasn't keen on visiting my father's friends and meeting a girl who was then only eight. Now if she had been *eighteen*! But she wasn't and there were plenty of girls who were, so I never turned up.

As an industrial chemist with one of the larger concerns, my father was interested in everything that touched his work. Peta's father was in the same line. He published an article in some learned journal that attracted Dad's interest, letters were exchanged and the first visit made.

That was twelve years ago. I don't remember when I first realised Dad was interested in women again. He had grown in on himself when my mother had died some years before, but suddenly he became sociable again. I seemed to hear nothing but talk of the Squire family. Perhaps that's why I never went near them – I was sick of the sound of them.

I'm quite sure Dad was attracted to Mrs Squire from the beginning but, as I said, there was nothing more than friendship between them, until five years ago. Peta's father had died very suddenly. A heart attack at his work. Naturally my father was at the Squire home a lot, doing what he could to help. I'd grown used by then to him being there. I took it for granted, and it was no real surprise when he told me he was going to marry Mrs Squire.

'If there's one thing certain in the world it's the fact that they were happy. Are they still? I simply don't know. Four years ago everything changed. They seem to me now to occupy separate little islands in a big river. Perhaps that sounds fanciful, but it's the best I can do, Marion, to describe it to you. They see one another and they exchange greetings and to outsiders they're a normal married couple, but I know my father so well, and he's drawn back in on himself again. She has, too. I'm sure of it. They're together in the stream of life about them, you see, but they don't touch anymore – they keep to their own little worlds, apart from civilised communication.

That's what those four years have done to them.

The first time I ever met Peta was when she was fifteen. She was a bridesmaid at the wedding. She wore a pale pink dress and a little flowered cap, and she was painfully correct and polite to everyone.

Only when the happy couple had gone off did she relax. I was the best man and she hadn't so much as looked at me up till then, but she swung round on me and said, 'Well, you've managed to meet me at last. Am I so utterly frightful?' and I realised that she must have taken it to heart that I'd never turned up at the house.

I asked her if that was so, and she said, 'Well, what do you imagine I thought? Every time you were asked over you developed a broken-down car, or bunions or measles or something.' She pulled a face at me and added, 'Sniff hard – I'm quite nice to be near, brother dear.'

She wasn't a bit ill-at-ease with me, and I enjoyed her chatter, but though I saw her from time to time after that there was a big gap between us – fifteen and twenty-five are worlds apart, as you'll realise yourself – and I was a fully-fledged pilot and travelling the world. I saw her only rarely in the next year, till I broke my ankle and had to stay home, and home of course was with my stepmother.

I had time and leisure to observe them all then and what I saw disturbed me. Dad and my stepmother were happy. There was no doubt about that, but somewhere something had gone wrong, and every time Dad entered the room Peta would become the painfully correct, painfully polite little creature of the wedding day. Dad wasn't much better and, I'm afraid to my amusement, I realised he was terrified of her, for the simple reason he had never before had a daughter. He'd been suddenly presented with one almost grown-up and he didn't have a clue how to treat her.

It tickled me, and it worried me, too, because it seemed both of them were missing out on something wonderful in not coming to an understanding of each other. I was still wondering if there wasn't something I could do about it, when school broke up, Christmas descended on us and the New Year too and then Peta went off on holiday.

She was looking forward to it immensely. I do know that. She had all sorts of plans, but the theme-song for her was the fun of finding a brand new companion on the trail.

Neither of the parents prevented her. Peta's mother is infinitely level-headed. I think it is an indication of the complete trust they both had in her that they made no objection – they knew she was level-headed, trustworthy, could stand on her own feet, could sum people up well and not get taken down by some unpleasant trickster, and that she wouldn't take up with a boy instead of another girl.

They trusted her completely to take care of herself, and I can't bring myself to believe Peta would have betrayed that trust by stooping to this souveniring business.

Certainly we read the press story of the two girls, but the name was given as Winchely. Certainly we heard and saw the other reports and learned the girl's name was Peta. Would *you* have jumped to the conclusion that Peta Winchely the trouble-maker, was Peta Squire, the girl we knew? It would have been crazy.

We were so far from realising the truth that Peta was in serious trouble that the parents went out that Sunday evening to visit friends. That's what that day was for us all – normal. The parents went out and I had a book and was learning to hobble around on crutches.

I've often wondered since what agony Peta went through while she was getting back to us. We learned afterwards that Sandra Kilby was fortunate enough to catch a train about to leave

Asherton and took it to the terminus and then managed to catch the express to Central. From there she took a taxi home and arrived in the early evening.

Peta wasn't so lucky. She wandered around in a state of shock for some time after leaving the park. By the time she had recovered her wits she was terrified of going anywhere near a station for fear the police were waiting to pick her up.

She was still wearing her dress and carrying the suitcase. She hitched a ride. She didn't look like a hitch-hiker, of course, and for her it was one ride after another till she reached home. Simply because she hadn't looked like the normal hitch-hiker she was picked up by one lift almost as soon as she left the previous one.

How she kept her composure through it all still leaves me bewildered, but to claim, as some people did afterwards, that she was a cool, calculating type who was fighting for her safety, and could think of nothing else, is wrong. I'm sure of it.

It must have been after eleven o'clock when she finally reached home. I was heading for bed and when the bell rang I thought the parents had forgotten their keys. I was going to tease them about it. Then I saw Peta.

She didn't say anything. She brushed past me and went straight to her room. I remember thinking she had a cool cheek and I went to demand how it happened her ladyship had returned home, and at that hour, too.

When I went into her room she looked up and she said quite simply, 'Ward, I'm in terrible trouble. There's a man dead. They'll probably say I did it.'

Well – it was simply unbelievable. Would *you* have believed that sort of yarn flung at you? Peta was a great one for telling tall yarns, delivered with a straight face.

I laughed, and asked where the punch line was, and then I stopped laughing. It was the look in her eyes. She looked as though I'd hit her, quite brutally and senselessly.

I asked her to tell me what was really wrong, but I'd hurt her too much. She said, 'I can't tell *you*. You always mock at everything I do or say.' She asked where her mother was, and when I told her there was the flash of the old Peta in the way she commanded me to get them home.

They'd told me before leaving that they might be home very late, but it didn't seem the time for waiting round. I mightn't have known much about girls of sixteen, but even I could tell Peta was about to break down completely. I rang the house where the parents were and when Dad came on the line I said, 'Come back at once. Peta is home and says there's bad trouble. She wants you.'

Dad must have broken the speed limit that night. They were walking through the front door ten minutes later and we got the whole story out of Peta. She was close to breaking down, remember, but her story was quite clear, with no fumbling, no signs she was selecting words with care and spinning a tissue of lies. it was the story she was to tell the police and stick to through all the questioning of the months ahead.

It was after midnight – a long time after, before we had ceased questioning her and knew all she could tell us. I remember that clearly, because later Inspector Podmore asked what time it was when Peta came home and told her story, and when I told him he said bluntly, 'Jack Burton died early that Sunday morning – very early. Before eight o'clock. Between then and midnight there were sixteen hours. That's a long time, Mr Wincham. What did Peta do in them besides finding her way home? Think, of course. And what did she think of in particular? Lies?

He was right, of course. Sixteen hours is a long time, but Podmore's thrust applies to Sandra too. It wasn't sixteen hours before she arrived home – something less, but she didn't, like Peta have to hitch a series of lifts. She was in trains most of the time, with ample opportunity and peace to think.

So it applies to them both. They both had time to think hard and decide what they were going to say before they had to face the questions.

Letter sent to Marion Burton:

Dear Miss Burton

I'm glad to know you heard from Mrs Kilby as I told you at our first interview I doubted very much if she would co-operate, but the copy you've sent me of her letter holds nothing at all that is new to me. I told you what to expect.

Ward Wincham is quite correct in his remembrance of the talk I had to him about the time lapse. I should have told you at our interviews that naturally we had searched for anyone who had seen the girls on their way home, and that actually everyone concerned came forward voluntarily. Of course, by then the case was an open sensation and, to put it quite brutally, I imagine bets were being freely laid in every pub in the state, as to which girl would eventually be pulled in. Everyone wanted to hand us the solution. The pity was that no one could.

The reason I failed to mention those people who came forward is simply that they had nothing to tell that cast the least light on our enquiries.

To take Sandra Kilby first – she went to the station and was lucky enough to catch a train to a country terminus. I imagine her state then was such that she would have stepped into the first train that came, regardless of its destination, but she was lucky. She was lucky again in the fact it was Sunday, that few people were travelling, and she must certainly have found an empty carriage. No one saw her on that train at all.

At the terminus she was noticed, but simply because she enquired if she could get a train there for Central. By that time it was two and a quarter hours after the death of Jack Burton. The boy – he was only eighteen himself – on duty that Sunday remembered her because she was left alone on the platform at the terminus and made no effort to leave and he thought she was a fare dodger and was waiting till he was out of sight before sneaking out the exit.

He went up to her in the end and that was when she made her enquiry. She didn't have a ticket. That wasn't remarkable. Only one man had been on duty at Asherton. He had closed the ticket office when the train was sighted, and gone to flag it in and out of the station. It would have been easy for Sandra to get through the barrier and on to the train without being noticed, as he had several parcels for the mail van at the back of the train.

At the terminus Sandra claimed her absence of ticket was due to her having arrived just in time to catch the train. She gave the name of a town three stops away from Asherton and made no bones about paying the boy. He then sold her a ticket to Central and saw her on to the Express. The terminus was a request stop only for the Express. The boy had to flag it down.

He remembered her quite well, for all those reasons, yet he was no help at all. She was quiet, polite, reserved and certainly not distraught and upset, but remember, she had had two and a quarter hours alone in the first train in which to compose herself and think what to do.

On the express there were people who noticed her, but only because the express stopped at the terminus, and she was the sole person to get into their carriage. At no time on that run to Central did she cause anyone to notice her for any other reason.

At Central she picked up a taxi. The driver says she seemed tired. That was all he could tell us. He saw her go up the path to the front door of the house and saw her go through the front door.

That is where certainty ends for us. We don't know and never will, I am sure, exactly what took place afterwards.

Then take Peta Squire. We have her story that she wandered around in a state of shock for a little while. This is borne out by the fact that she didn't hitch her first ride for a couple of hours after Jack Burton's death. She claims she cannot remember exactly where she went in the interval – she simply avoided people and went on moving away from the park, out of Asherton.

All we know is that it was a lost two hours before she hitched that first lift. Two hours remember – almost the same stretch of time that Sandra Kilby had before she was first seen and had to talk to anyone.

That first driver, who took her from the outskirts of Asherton, could say only that the girl complained of a bad headache, asked to be driven as far as possible in the direction of the city and then leaned back and closed her eyes. The woman was disappointed. She had wanted company, but she accepted Peta's silence.

That report was echoed by all other drivers that day. Peta seemed tired, she gave as little information as possible about her journey and reason for hitch-hiking, and seemed to wish to sleep.

And like Sandra Kilby, she was seen to go up a path and through a front door, and that was the last certain fact we had.

You asked me several times to say which was the one youngster I thought was lying. I told you I never decided. That's the simple truth. Nowhere even in their characters could I find a positive clue. Peta was a sensible, normally intelligent and normally behaved girl who got on well with people, was used to hitch-hiking, had maturity and commonsense and the ability to look after herself. Sandra was a shy, well-behaved and quite popular girl, of normal intelligence, who was making her first attempt to untie her mother's apron strings.

I can't say which of them might have been the one who started the souveniring.

Sandra's teachers say she was left out of many things, due to her mother's influence. She might have sought for popularity, status, and equality for instance, by accepting a dare to bring back a collection of souvenirs to equal or better those collected by others.

Peta's teachers say she was the type to be impatient of a dare; that she would feel no need to prove herself to anyone. All I have heard about her and my own talks to her convince me that is quite correct, but – it is a plain fact that if a child's life is suddenly upset, if they have suffered a loss, if they feel deprived in some way, they may take to stealing. I've had a talk with doctors. They've convinced me. Deprivation of one thing can make them seek solace in the hoarding and collection of possessions. Stealing, so I'm informed, can also be unstated cries on the part of the child that the people who are apparently neglecting it should notice it, even if only to deal out punishment. I've been cited enough cases to prove the point to convince me there is something in it.

You might say Peta is not a child, but she was an adolescent and suffered the usual torments of that state, I imagine, and, in two short years she had lost her father, she had seemingly lost her mother to a new husband and this new husband was not someone who apparently took much interest in Peta. Her home was suddenly, as she had said to one teacher, a place where there seemed to be guests to dinner every night. In other words she had lost her father, her usual home life, and her mother, in one fell swoop. Even the new step-brother ignored her – he was the man who had developed car trouble, or bunions or measles every time he had been invited to meet her!

Given all that, the doctors think it quite feasible she might have suddenly started to collect possessions, to steal them and hoard them. They say she might have wanted to take them home and find out just what the reaction would be to her behaviour. She might have wanted everyone's attention and interest, however unpleasant the end result.

Even the items taken proved to be of no help. Remembering the doctor's statements, I took a long look at them. The ashtray was the sort of item that *is* souvenired, and the taking of unusual car mascots is commonplace, but the knife and the pill box? They were left where anyone could take them, but they hardly class as souvenirs. It might have been that Peta Squire had become a compulsive taker of anything available.

Equally, though, Sandra Kilby, looking for anything and as many things as possible, to bring back as souvenirs to overshadow the collection of other girls, might grab at anything that was easily available for taking.

So you see, there was no help in their characters either. After all the questioning and seeking of help, we were left with the simple fact – one perfectly ordinary schoolgirl stepped out of normal character and took something that wasn't hers and in taking set in motion a landslide that finished in your brother's death.

Sincerely, Larry Podmore

15

The day had begun with pouring rain. Jefferson Shields stood watching the wash of it down the street, and the procession of figures wrapped against the weather, who came walking past. He was thinking of that other wet day in another January when a procession of figures, 'wrapped like cellophane packages' had come down a hill from a hostel.

He didn't move from his contemplation till he saw the woman in the red raincoat turn in through the doorway to the building. He turned then, went back to his desk and said, 'You can show Miss Burton straight in, Mrs Gold.'

When she came in, it was with the red raincoat over her arm. She was wearing a sleeveless dress again, with no concession to the day – a beige silk-like sheath with a facing of big copper buttons.

He said, without preamble, 'You're afraid that Ward Wincham is the one who lied.'

Her cheeks reddened. For a minute she looked angry, and he thought she was going to lash out at him with unguarded tongue, then she dropped into the chair, reached for a cigarette and said shortly, 'I suppose it was obvious. Ward was alone in the house when Peta came home. There's only his word she didn't tell her story until the others came back.'

'What is the real relationship between them? Then – and through the years – and now?' He sat down behind the desk, waiting patiently.

Her tongue betrayed her. She was irritated and angry at having to answer. 'I don't know. I simply don't *know*. Oh, I think it's correct that they were just, well, the products of two marriages thrown together because of their parents. Maybe they even resented each other a bit. Ward says not on his part. He just wasn't interested in her. His father was content. That was all that mattered to Ward.

'Then afterwards, when all the trouble started, of course he took a different view. He *had* to be interested. He points that out himself. His family, he himself, were all involved. He did what he could to help, to encourage, to probe. It was natural for Peta to lean on the help, while resenting the probing.

'Ward calls it a sort of neutrality between them – neither close friendship nor dislike. Ward was necessary to her for a while. She was grateful that he helped. She has remained grateful. Ward visits her when he's home. She makes no objection. She cooks dinner for him and goes to great pains over it, so he says. She draws him out on the places he sees in his job – he's still with the airline, and still flying overseas. She seems interested, and to enjoy his visits.'

She shrugged, 'That's all.'

'And her relationship, now, with her mother and Mr Wincham?'

She hesitated, drew deeply on the cigarette, considered the glowing tip of it for a long silent moment, then said, 'The same, I think – I mean, the same attitude as to Ward. She is grateful to them for standing by. She visits them. They occasionally dine with her in her flat.' She leaned forward, stubbing out the cigarette with a force that split it, leaving it an ugly, untidy thing in the hollow of the golden glass. She demanded, 'Which of them lied?'

When he didn't answer, she went on impatiently, 'It's not Ward. Don't you see Peta could have had her story ready and Ward could have accepted, but later on he was well again, and he had to go back to work. Peta was alone with her parents and the police. The latter were questioning all the time. Can you imagine that Peta's mother and Ward's father didn't question, too? If they found something that seemed wrong – oh, don't you see they could have realised she was lying, but they wouldn't tell?' she assured him.

'I wasn't lying to you yesterday. I must know whether they helped her lie, and Ward, too,' she said. 'But as it is, it's impossible for me to grow closer to Ward, too – '

'Has he asked you to marry him?' he demanded.

The answer was in her face, but she said, 'No. You must realise yourself how it is – I'm Jack's sister. What's going to happen if he thrust *me* into the family? It would be unbearable for them, unbearable for me. Apart from everything else, Ward's devoted to his father. He might make light of it, but he is. He likes Peta's mother, too, though I don't think they're close – just two people who have a mutual interest – which is Mr Wincham, of course.'

She moved impatiently. 'The whole thing's impossible. Maybe you're sitting there and telling yourself that I must have been short-sighted not to see all this in the beginning – that I should have kept well clear of Ward and never become involved with him but, you see, I was Jack's sister, and he was Peta's step-brother. We couldn't keep away from each other. There was a mutual curiosity, a – don't you understand what I mean?'

'Yes, certainly. It was inevitable you should draw together instead of moving apart. No one ever takes the wiser course when curiosity urges them to take another.' He told her abruptly, 'I need to see Peta and – '

'I guessed that.' The dark head nodded vigorously. She was pleased, he could see, that she had forestalled him in something. 'Ward's talked her into seeing you. She didn't want to, of course, but he's home and he's talked to her. They'll both be at her flat. All day.'

She was standing up, pulling on the red raincoat, taking it for granted that he was ready to come immediately. He made no protest.

He was a crow-like figure beside her red raincoat – with a long, black, crumpled plastic raincoat and a black hat. he was shorter than the girl too, but his stride was surprisingly long, and he made no effort to find a taxi.

She resented that, skipping through the puddles at his side, but he appeared to see no oddity in them striding through the downpour. Instead he went on questioning her, demanding, 'Have you made any attempt to see Sandra Kilby, or her parents?'

'I rang once. I had the address and the number was in the book. I rang. It was Mrs Kilby, or Smith – whatever you like to call her who answered. When I gave my name the line was dead.

'I rang the hotel where Sandra works, too. The same thing happened. I had a letter the next day. It was from a firm of solicitors. As Ward said, it boiled down to "Lay off, or else!"

'I don't blame them,' she added, 'and after all they've said all they wanted to and had to a thousand times already. 'What,' she demanded, 'are you going to ask Peta that hasn't been asked a hundred times, too?'

The grey eyes blinked at her from the shelter of the grey rimmed spectacles. There was a spatter of raindrops on the glass, but he didn't seem to notice. He said mildly, 'I don't know.'

He knew she was disappointed and angry with him, and the fact faintly amused him for a moment, then was forgotten, because they had turned into a street lined with small shops of the type that are handed down from work-weary parents to sons, and on to grandsons, without anything more than a bare living being ever scratched out of them.

Marion paused at a doorway between two shopfronts. It was painted bright blue, the number 15 was enamelled in white. She pushed it open, and they faced the narrow concrete treads of uncarpeted stairs. The space was gloomy, there was a strong smell of cheese and spiced sausage and there was a square of white tacked to wood on the banister. It said baldly, in black scrawl, 'Do not leave any articles on stairs or banisters.'

Apologetically, Marion said, 'There are two flats. The owners – the people who run the delicatessen down there – have one. Peta has the other.'

At the top of the stairs was a narrow landing, almost filled with a bright blue pot in which an orchid plant thrived lushly. Marion knocked on the door to the left of it. She was already pulling off the red raincoat.

The man who filled the opened doorway was unexpected. Jefferson Shields had imagined him as the pilots he had known in the long ago war – a slim, dapper figure. This man was big, firmly muscled, with a stong heavy jaw and eyes that in the half light, seemed to glint green.

He stood aside without comment. Marion rushed into breathless speech, but he stopped her with a crisp, 'I'm glad you came early.' He held out a hand to the other man, as he said in that same clipped, crisp tone, 'I'm Ward Wincham.'

He led the way down the narrow hall, into a room at the end.

Jefferson Shields's impression was of whiteness. After the gloom of the stairs and landing it was blinding. White blazed at him from ceiling and walls and furniture. Only when the first dazzle had receded did he make out the muted tones of the striped cushions – browns and dulled orange and greyed-greens – that blended in with the dulled brown of the carpet. The woman was in white, too.

It was with a sense of something close to outrage that he looked at her, because after all those words he had read and sifted through the previous day and night he had had her in mind's eye – a thin wraith of a girl with sunburned skin and long dark brown hair.

This woman was a total stranger. Her skin was creamy white. Against it her deep-set eyes blazed blue under the short-cropped shining dark hair and her body – if she had ever been a thin clown-like figure who had danced through the dust to Asherton, there was no sign of it now. Her body, and her white dress was a sheathed one as tight-fitting as Marion's own, was perfectly formed.

It was a woman's voice that spoke to him, too. The deep tones were still there, but it held maturity and a richness that it could never have held four years before.

She said, 'Sit down, Mr Shields.' Then she added, the blue eyes holding his own gaze in dismissal, 'You've come to question me, and I've agreed to let you do it, but it will be useless. You'll learn nothing.'

A warning? He wondered that and if she was telling him he could never break her story, or that she had long ago accepted that nothing would help her.

He had told Marion Burton quite honestly that he didn't know what he would ask her. He had wanted to see her, and he knew now he had been hoping to see in her face some clue as to how the years in between had used her, and how she had used them.

He looked round the small room. It was elegant, it was tasteful and almost impersonal. There were no photos, no trinkets, no memory at all of that other January. He wondered what she had done with the rucksack, and the postcards she had bought in the store where the knife was stolen.

Abruptly he asked, 'What happened to the road bible?'

She was startled. Her lips parted and for a moment she was silent. Then she said, 'It's odd – no one has asked me that, ever before.'

'Do you know the answer?'

'No. I expect Sandra destroyed it. She must have, mustn't she?' She eyed him thoughtfully. 'If her story was to hold together she must have destroyed it. It's queer I never once thought of it.' A frown gathered and grew across her forehead, then smoothed away. She said, half impatiently now, 'But the police would naturally have asked about it. They didn't find it. That's obvious.'

The crisp voice demanded from the other side of the room, 'What was the purpose of the question?'

Jefferson Shields blinked. He said mildly, almost apologetically, 'I don't really know. It just popped into my head.'

Surprisingly, Peta laughed, and the sound held genuine amusement. She said, 'Well, you're a change. All of them so far have been, well, god-like, throwing questions at me as though they held unknown depths and traps; that there were whole hosts of things they knew and were waiting for me to admit.' She added, the amusement gone, 'I felt surrounded by gods who had sat on Olympian heights and had studied everything I did, and knew everything and were toying with me – '

'Waiting for you to admit the truth?'

She laughed again. 'No. Don't try to be too clever, Mr Shields. I kept waiting for them to say, instead, that they knew quite well I was innocent. That's quite true. I kept expecting them to do something brilliant and prove that my story was the only feasible one. Only they didn't.'

'Did you go back and complete your normal schooling?'

'Now, I wonder what made you ask that?' There was half mockery in the deep-set blue eyes. 'Did it just pop into your head, too? No, I didn't go. It would have been quite unbearable. Oh, not because a lot of people would have shunned me. I don't think I would have honestly cared about that.' Her head tilted as she surveyed that point, then she gave a short nod. 'No, I think I'd just have said – well, you're entitled to your opinion – and left them to their own devices, but there's another type of person who likes to touch the fringes of disaster, who likes to be in there in case something dramatic happens and they can coyly say, "But I knew her well. We shared sandwiches and confidences often." You must know the type I mean. I didn't fancy being taken up by them.'

The slender shoulders lifted and fell in a quick shrug. 'In any case, I wasn't much of a scholar. I don't mean I landed bottom of the class with monotonous regularity. My mother laid down standards she knew I could keep with the brains I possessed.' She smiled at him. 'If I slipped below those standards I could expect trouble, but they were quite reachable.

'I rather enjoyed school, but quite honestly I didn't weep

too much when it was over. There' – her eyes mocked him again – 'don't say I don't answer your questions fully.'

He said dryly, 'Too fully. You're hoping a spate of words will tire me, use up time; so that we'll never reach down and touch anything that you *don't* wish to discuss.'

The creamy-white of her skin flushed red – the blush extending to her slim throat. It deepened still further as the man's laughter came from the other side of the room.

She said at last, 'You're clever.' Her gaze was intent, the mockery gone.

He asked equably, 'What *don't* you wish to discuss? You might as well tell me and then I won't have to waste time prying, while you sit there on edge, hoping I'll never reach it.'

She said again, 'You're clever,' and the deep voice held surprise. After a moment she said levelly, 'I don't want to talk about Sandra. When I do, I can't see other things in proper perspective. It's as though she's there all the time in front of me, mouthing her own story at me, and I can't think properly.' She looked down at her slim hands, clasped in the lap of the white dress. 'I expect that sounds as though I'm the one who lied – that conscience gets between me and the lies when I'm trying to say them, reminding of the true story – hers.'

He didn't speak, and she went on at last, after a sharp puzzled glance at him, 'I don't want to talk about Jack Burton either.' She flashed one look towards Marion and away again. 'It's a curious thing, but until I saw his photo in the press afterwards, I didn't know what he looked like at all. I know that sounds crazy, but it's true. He was just a blur, shoving in between us.'

'If your story is true, Sandra had that knife a couple of days, yet you never saw it?'

'I didn't see that shell ashtray either. I wouldn't have seen that car mascot, except that she showed it to me. Why should I have seen the knife? I didn't go searching through her rucksack, you know.'

'Not even when you new about the pill box? Didn't you think there might be other things she had taken?'

Her small even teeth bit into her lower lip. Then she said, 'Oh, I thought of it all right. I just didn't want to know for sure. It would have been the last straw if I'd found other things. I'd have lost my temper, and there would have been a flaming row that nothing would have smoothed over. Even when old Mr Bossley made the police start looking for us – well, she'd agreed to go home, you see. I just didn't want to know what else she might have that wasn't her own property.'

'Have you – *did* you, have a bad temper? You've just mentioned the danger of losing it.'

She answered without hesitation, 'Quite bad when I was worked up enough about something to really let fly. Usually I couldn't be so concerned about things that I felt deeply involved, deeply betrayed or angered.' She shook her head. 'But I would have been all those if Sandra had wanted to tell the police and I was afraid of the results, wouldn't I? So it's possible I could have let fly with both temper and a knife, there in Asherton Park.' After a long silence she added, 'It's quite useless. You must be realising it yourself. There are two ways of looking at every last single thing in the whole mess.'

Shields moved slowly, so that he could see the tall man leaning against the corner wall. In the light of the white room the eyes didn't look so green, but the impression of strength and hardness remained, even when the man smiled at him and said gently, 'Well?'

He might have been tossing a ball lightly towards the other man in a game. Shields tossed it back with, 'When Peta came home that night, exactly what did she say to you? I want the exact words, if you can remember.'

The dark brows went up. 'I can remember. She walked past without a word and went to her own room. I followed her in, and asked why she'd come home. She said, "Ward, I'm in terrible trouble. There's a man dead. They'll probably say I did it."'

'Why? Why should they? What made her think that anyone would blame her for it? What made her think that Sandra wouldn't be caught, wouldn't confess?' Shields's

voice held puzzlement. 'Hasn't anyone questioned how completely senseless that statement is, if the girl who said it was
innocent?'

'You've done your homework,' the big man said. The
green seemed deeper in the wide-set eyes, as though there was
excitement in the thought behind them. He said, 'Of course, it
was noticed. The police jumped on it at once, pointing out
that for all Peta knew, if her story was true, Sandra might have
been caught at the very moment she was first speaking to me.

'Only, you see, there was an answer. The very last thing
Peta did before she came home was listen to the late news on
the radio, in the last car of her trip home. You see, they
announced the death of Jack Burton – but there was no mention of Sandra, no mention of anything except that the reason
for his death was *unknown*.

'She knew, you understand.' There was a pity so deep in
the man's voice that Shields lifted his head and looked at him
with new attention. The pity went ringing round the small
room as he added, 'When she walked up that path in through
the door she knew that Sandra hadn't confessed, and hadn't
been caught. She had run away from that horrible scene
because she didn't want to be there when Sandra was caught.
She didn't want to be questioned and have to condemn
Sandra. She ran away from that. She ran away to us here,
wanting us with her when the police did finally arrive. She was
sure they'd arrive you see, because she was sure Sandra would
be caught and would tell everything about the whole journey
towards Asherton.

'She listened to that radio because she wanted to find out if
the police already knew where she lived; if they'd be waiting
for her when she walked through the door. She wanted to
have herself braced to face them and then – she realised
Sandra had run away, too. She was terribly, utterly frightened
then. Can't you understand her state of mind? She was sure
the police would trace them, eventually, but what was Sandra
going to say?

'There had been only the two of them, and Sandra never took the blame for anything. Peta had found that out a dozen times. Sandra would go to any length to prove that she was never to blame for anything that went wrong. Peta remembered and she wondered what if Sandra refused to take the blame for Burton's death?

'With all that in her head and heart, wasn't it obvious she should say to me, "There's a man dead. They'll probably say I did it."'

He took a step forward, towering over the seated man.

'That girl would never take or accept the blame for anything! I told them – the police – that. I said to them, "Go to her parents, her teachers, her schoolmates and their parents and demand the truth off them about that. Make them admit Sandra'd do anything to prove that she was never in the wrong." She wasn't capable of shouldering blame, of shrugging it off, of accepting punishment. She had neither the maturity nor the self-confidence for it.'

The voice stopped. One big hand went to his dark head. He stepped back. His voice had dropped from its great thundering shout to its normal tones when he added, 'They asked. It was a blank wall. I don't know why. Perhaps some people couldn't remember examples to quote, or had never been present when they'd happened, but I think – I'm pretty sure, in fact, that a lot of them didn't want to admit it. The teachers, in particular. You see, to admit it, was to cast the first doubt on Sandra's word, and there was no more doubt we could find to add to it. So why admit to it? Why admit the faintest doubt that might rub off on the school and the rest of the students?

'It wouldn't, you see, be politic to admit they might have taught or rubbed shoulders with a girl who could have caused such trouble. If there'd been other doubts it would have been different. As it was, it was a case of thinking of the school and the other students first.

'You can't blame them, I suppose, but – ' He shook his head. 'So it came down in the end to there being only Peta's word about that, too. The police said she could have made it up to show that Sandra wouldn't take blame for the stealing, or killing, either.' His voice swept back in a raging gust that hit at the white walls. 'And when they couldn't find proof that Sandra was like that, it came back to – why did Peta say that to me – that she'd probably get blamed herself?

'It was a see-saw,' he said impatiently. 'One minute it would seem that Sandra was down and Peta on top and the next the mass of words weighted down the other end and Peta was down and Sandra on top.'

He demanded, 'What else have you got to ask?'

'Why, if you believed Peta's story, didn't you immediately contact the police that Sunday night?'

'Because of the radio story, of course – the death was a *mystery*. Sandra had run away. Do you think we *wanted* Peta to have to tell her story if it wasn't necessary? We were praying it wouldn't ever be necessary. The reports kept coming over the air and in the press that it was still a mystery, so we waited.'

He asked again, 'What else?'

'Have any of you – your father, stepmother, Peta or your-self – seen Sandra or her parents?'

Peta said sharply, violently, 'No!'

Over the denial came Ward's voice, 'No, but I did have a shot at seeing them. I wanted to see what they were like and perhaps talk to them and Sandra but, of course, it was no good. I went a couple of times. After the last I had a solicitor's letter. It told me to stay away; that any communication I wished to send could go through them. That was all. I didn't bother answering. There was no point in it. I'd wanted to see them all, speak to them, weigh them up.'

'Appeal to them?'

'Yes, that, of course, but the answer was obvious. If she were guilty they'd be frightened that I'd trip her up; if inno-cent that I'd try confusing her and tripping her just the same, for my own ends.'

He demanded again, 'What else have you got to ask?'

Jefferson Shields stood up. He said gently, 'Nothing. It was, of course, and I think you realise it, to see you in the flesh that I came here. Questions at this point are hardly sensible. If Peta is innocent, she has told everything she knows. If not, she would be careful to tell nothing more than she has done already.'

Peta stood up and came close to him. She said, 'Thank you for being honest. So many people haven't been, you see. They've flattered me, and they've offered false hope and they've smiled false smiles that don't reach their eyes and – I'm so *tired* of it!'

He looked back from the bottom of the dark stairway. She was standing in the open doorway, a figure of light in the white dress against the light from the open door behind. Ward bulked large, formidable, watchful, behind her.

Outside on the pavement Marion said sharply, eagerly, the anxiety plain in her voice and face, 'What do you think of Ward?'

He looked at her levelly, 'That he is a very ruthless man.'

'Ruth – ?' She stared at him. 'I wonder why you think so.' Then anxiety grew, 'Do you mean that you think he lied? That he'd be ruthless enough to – '

He broke across the words, 'You told me that you rang the hotel where Sandra Kilby, or Smith works? You must have the address. Would she be at work now?'

'Yes. She works from eight to four. What are you going to do if she has you thrown off the premises?' There was a faint malicious amusement in the question.

He reproved her, 'That was hardly an intelligent question. She has her job under an assumed name. Is it likely she would cause a scene, demand the removal of someone who was likely to state her real name and to say, in public, why they had come to see her?'

16

He was reminded at once of that statement in which Inspector Podmore had spoken of the first time he had ever seen Sandra Kilby. Of that day he had written, 'She was cool, calm, composed.'

The woman who looked up at them and watched them approach over the parquet floor of the reception hall was all that. If Peta Squire had grown into a strikingly attractive woman, Sandra Kilby was close to being a beautiful one. Either she had never cut the long fair hair of four years before, or she had cut it and had the long plait made into a fall, because her small head was crowned with luxuriant fairness.

That she was considered an asset to the hotel, he was sure. Her smile was reserved but welcoming. It revealed excellent teeth and a small dimple in her chin.

He was reminded of the descriptions of her that talked of her innocent grey eyes. They still held that innocence, and remoteness too. They surveyed him and Marion with politeness, but no warmth, in spite of her smiling mouth.

Few people though, he was sure, would have noticed that the eyes never smiled. To the casual guest she would be a charming introduction to the premises.

Her voice was good, too. Neither too loud nor too soft, and quite accentless, so that she could have been of any nationality, any class. It was as unrevealing as the name of Smith that she had adopted.

She asked them, 'You have a reservation?' and the inno-cent, remotely unsmiling eyes summed them up. Shields was sure she had priced his own suit and crumpled raincoat and Marion's simple sheath of a dress and expensive red macin-tosh to the last cent and that she was already neatly pigeon-holing them into one of the hotel's rooms.

He answered, 'No, Miss Kilby.'

For a moment her smile remained. Her gaze went to the open book in front of her, then lifted again. She surveyed him coolly. 'Just who are you?' Her voice had hardened quite noticeably.

He told her. She answered the name and waited for him to add to it. He told her almost apologetically, 'I deal in puzzles. In presenting a solution to them.'

Whatever reaction he had expected it wasn't a sigh of resignation. She said, 'You're the – let's see – the eleventh, I think. I've almost lost count, and that's merely the ones who've come to me. Some have gone to my father, and some to my mother, but I suppose I'm regarded as being the easiest touch.'

He stared at her. 'Do you mean people come to you and say that they can solve the puzzle of four years ago? You do mean that, don't you?'

'Of course.' A quick gesture of her hand dismissed him utterly. 'I don't know what price you're offering, but the cheapest so far has been one hundred dollars. Cash, of course.

'Actually I don't think the police would have been flattered by that. If the case could have been solved by a mere one hun-dred dollars worth of extra work, they would surely have put in a few extra hours on it themselves.'

It was Marion who broke the silence. She said, 'I'm Jack Burton's sister.'

The shock wave of it seemed to mould the oval face into new contours, flattening and widening the mouth and nar-rowing the grey eyes. For a minute Jefferson Shields thought she was going to give a furious denial to the statement, then she said, 'I recognise you now! I saw your photos. A lot of them.' Her voice reproached, 'You wrote to my mother and she answered. Against her better judgment. Against my father's too. They took your letter to our solicitors. They wanted advice and help and all Mr Barclay could do was tell them to answer. He said if they did you'd not bother us again. If they didn't you'd only continue pestering. So my mother answered.' The reproach grew, 'Why come here?' Her gaze slid side-ways, 'And who *is* he?'

Marion said, 'He told you. I've asked him to tell me which one of you lied.'

She thought instantly, I shouldn't have said that. So baldly. So cruelly. It was unnecessary. She wanted to take the words back and substitute something else, but the other girl didn't seem upset by them.

She said only, 'He won't be able to tell you.' She lifted her gaze to Marion's. 'You'll waste a whole lot of money. You could use it for better things.' She demanded, 'What does it matter to you which of us lied? He's *dead*,' Her voice rolled with the shock of the word, as though it was only now she was realising the fact, or realising it all over again in a new shock wave. 'Inspector Podmore wrote to my mother and said that you'd become friendly with Peta's family. We thought it sounded impossible. How *could* you have become friendly with them?' There was real curiosity in the question and her wait-ing expression.

'Because I met Ward Wincham and we had a lot in com-mon and – there were things we shared – '

Sandra's teeth showed in a tight little smile. She said acidly, 'Like remembrances of four years ago? It doesn't sound like the sort of thing that would bring people together. It doesn't sound reasonable. I think you *made* an occasion to meet him, and get to know them. Why?' Her voice probed, 'Why do you want to know *now*?'

Marion was silent. She had the impression that if she answered, 'I want Ward to ask me to marry him,' the other girl would have regarded it not as much impossible, as ridiculous and laughable.

Jefferson Shield broke the silence, asking, 'What happened to the little book you called a road bible?'

She laughed. He was reminded of Peta's laughter, of the half mockery in Peta's eyes, as she said, 'Was that expected to trip me? My dear man, after the experience I've had of people throwing questions willy-nilly into my face, I couldn't possibly trip, however guilty. I'm quite, quite certain that the same applies to Peta Squire. By now we're conditioned – hardened, if you care to put it that way – to never being surprised at anything, never upset by anything. When the months go by you have to learn to be like a net across a court. The balls fly wickedly at you and they hit you, but you're tempered to meet them and they bounce off you without harming you.'

Her eyes held contempt now. 'Didn't you realise that for yourself? Didn't you ever consider that after four years the guilty one is hardened by guilt, and the innocent shielded by innocence? Haven't you reflected that by now practice must have made perfect, that we could recite our stories and stick to them without real thought of what we are saying? Did you honestly consider you could come to either of us and ask a question that had never been asked before? There aren't any left to ask!' The bitter admission was thrust at them in ever-rising contempt.

'You're a fool!' The contempt lashed at Marion with no pity. 'If he's told you he can give you an answer he's taking your money under false pretences.'

'I can't blame her.' Marion's voice held apology both for the admission and for Sandra's contempt.

'Oh no,' he nodded quickly, 'her reaction was quite natural. That was interesting, what she told us, of people offering to solve the case, for a fee. Were the Wincham family approached in the same fashion?'

'Yes.' She sounded puzzled. 'Inspector Podmore told them it was the usual thing in such a case – that all the ghouls in the world saw in them a chance of easy money. Although Ward says he thought one or two were genuine. Genuine, at least, in believing they could help. Only they were mental cases. They claimed to be able to have visions – you must know the type of person I mean?'

'Yes. They appear pathetic. Actually they can be very dangerous, because they can mislead, distort facts, raise hopes that are later shattered.'

She considered that thoughtfully, her gaze on the pouring rain. He had led her, without comment, to the shelter of a bus seat under one of the shop awnings. She felt awkwardly exposed to everyone's sight and hearing there, but he seemed quite unconcerned.

She said at last, 'I expect you're right, if you don't see through them. You'd have to be a bit touched yourself to deal with them in the first place, wouldn't you?'

'Or desperate. Desperate people take to desperate measures. Did the Wincham family ever approach a private agency of their own accord, and ask for an investigation?'

'Yes. Peta's mother had no money of her own, and Mr Wincham had nothing saved, but there was Ward. I don't mean he had money. He had always spent everything he earned, but he borrowed on his future salary – a pilot on an overseas line make a big income, you know – and he went to a detective agency. It was a good one. They were honest, too. They read everything and they went to see the police. Afterwards they told Ward any investigation they could make would only parallel police enquiries – that he would be wasting his money.

'He went to another. They had other ideas.' Her voice had hardened. 'Oh, they held out no hope of doing better than the police, but they suggested faked evidence. For a price, of course.'

'And did Ward accept?'

Her whole expression and voice expressed rage and indignation as she flared at him, 'What have you against Ward? You dislike him! You've already told me you consider him a really ruthless man, but how could you possibly think for a minute anyone could stoop – '

He lifted a hand. He said, 'Be quiet.'

It was said quite softly, but it stopped her more effectively than if he had hit her. There was command in it and a faint contempt that made her look away.

He said, 'I've already pointed out that desperate people take desperate measures. Ward Wincham is a ruthless man. I am sure of that. Why, if he considered Peta innocent, and was certain of it in his heart, should he baulk at cornering the guilty girl through faked evidence? He would consider it merely furthering the cause of justice. Well?'

She said helplessly, 'You mean, of course, that he didn't think Peta innocent at all, that perhaps he knew she lied.' Her gaze returned to the driving rain and the wet street, then she said sharply, 'But it works both ways! Don't you see that it does? Look, if he knew Peta was lying and was ruthless enough to back her up in those lies and leave Sandra under the shadow of guilt, wouldn't he be ruthless enough to go ahead and condemn her utterly, and clear Peta altogether?' Impatiently she thrust at him, 'Your argument's quite unsound.'

'No. You're wrong. Ward Wincham is ruthless, but he is far from being a fool. He's a pilot. He is a man trained to being decisive, to using his wits and all caution in the face of danger, to seeing, quickly and efficiently, all round a possibly dangerous situation and taking prompt and efficient action to combat it.

'Faked evidence has a way of rebounding on the person who faked it. Inspector Podmore would tell you that. No policeman would have accepted suddenly appearing evidence without regarding it suspiciously and thoroughly investigating it. It is almost certain that in the end they would discover it was faked, and who did the job and how much was paid for the faking and which person paid the sum.

'The end result would have been harm to Peta's cause, not help for it – *if* Ward knew she was guilty. If she were innocent, though, the fakery might be exposed in the end, but in the interval the faked evidence would be thrown in the face of the girl who was guilty. It would be totally unexpected, disastrous, terrible and quite demoralising, because she wouldn't know that it might be exposed in the end as a fake. Under the strain of facing the unexpected she might well collapse and reveal the true story.'

He said very decidedly, 'I think Ward Wincham would have considered the risks, and decided they were justified – if he had known Peta was innocent, or was even certain enough of it to his own mind. If you question him now, I think he will tell you that is exactly how he reasoned. He will admit it, and it will tell you what you wanted to learn from me, because he will be admitting that he has never discovered if Peta lied or told the truth. You will know, quite definitely, that if she lied, that if her parents lied with her, Ward himself has no knowledge and certainty of it. He still knows no more than you do.'

He could see her hands clenching tighter and tighter. Abruptly they relaxed. She said, 'I still must know which one lied, and which parents.'

'Very well.' He stood up. He said, 'We will go and see Mrs Kilby.'

She shook her head, 'You'll merely get the door slammed in your face once she knows who we are and – '

'No.' He considered the point and rejected it with decision. 'By now, if Mrs Kilby is at home, she will have been phoned by Sandra. She will have been told that we have been to the hotel, that her mother must expect a visit. Her mother will be prepared. She will know that slamming the door in our faces will be senseless – we might return through the window, or put people to spy on her.' A faint smile touched his eyes as he turned to Marion. 'I think her reaction will be to phone Mr

Kilby. Didn't you notice that Sandra mentioned that your letter to Mrs Kilby was taken to Mr Kilby and then to the solicitors? The family still turns to Mr Kilby for advice when threatened. I think that by the time we reach there Mr Kilby will have been contacted. Either he will be with his wife or he will arrive shortly afterwards. They will expect us to go there, to the mother, when we have left the daughter.

'We might as well do the expected. It will save time.'

'What are you going to ask them?' She said, 'You admit yourself, to everyone, you're just asking the first things that come to mind. You've no plan at all!'

'Why should I have?' He gazed at her in honest surprise. 'I don't know these people as they are *now*. I have a good impression of them as they were four years ago. They couldn't possibly be the same people now as they were then. How do I know what to ask until I see them as they are today?'

Marion didn't know whether to laugh or show dismay. She walked in silence at his side, resenting again the fact that he was content to walk and not get a taxi, but the journey was short. Sandra had chosen her job only a short distance from the big new-looking apartment block where she and her mother had made their home on the fourth floor.

There was no doorman, and no lift driver. The place had an impersonal air that extended to the front doors of each apartment. Each painted in the same dulled beige shade, with chrome numbers affixed to mid-panel, they each had a small apologetic green plant spindling up from a small sandy-beige pot.

Shields had the irreverent thought that the God of the building department had waved his hand and decreed: Let there be plants, and lo, there had been plants in impersonal struggle for survival, without beginning or end.

Then the door marked 4D opened. The woman who stood there was small-boned, and short. Her dark hair was streaked with grey. Only the eyes were like Sandra's. They blazed at him from the sallowed, sagging lines of her face.

She said in something near triumph, 'Sandra guessed you would immediately come round here. Didn't she make it plain to you, Miss Burton?' She took a step forward, denying them any entrance. 'Can't you understand facts when they are presented to you plainly? Or didn't you hear clearly? She told you that every question possible had been asked us. Can't you accept that?'

Marion stared back wordlessly. Her eyes signalled to her companion, do something, for heaven's sake, or the door's going to close.

Jefferson Shields's head, in the wet balk hat, poked forward. He asked, 'What private enquiry agencies did you ask to investigate the case?'

'What?' The woman stared at him. She said sharply, 'We didn't employ anyone.' A frown creased deep lines across the sallow forehead. She said, 'Oh, I see what you mean – you're thinking of those – they were filth!' Her eyes burned at him in bitter anger. 'They hounded us. Did Sandra tell you about them? They pressed round the doors. They put notices *under* the doors, and rang us up and accosted us immediately we set foot outdoors. It was never-ending for a long time. Some of them didn't mean any harm – I think a few were mental cases. One woman claimed she would raise a spirit who would be able to find a witness on the other side, as she called it, who saw the stabbing. She said there were always spirits on the other side who had seen every crime on earth!' Her voice was shaking.

'We had nothing to do with any of them. Every time we had another letter, another caller, someone who rang up or accosted us, we took their name. We added we were giving it immediately to the police, to have the pest investigated with the possibility of having them charged with attempted fraud.'

She stopped. She said then quite clearly, 'As my husband will certainly have you investigated, Mr Shields. Sandra took your name. She has found your address in the phone book.'

There was triumph in her smile and in her backing away, and the way her hand reached for the door, to close it.

Jefferson Shields said mildly, 'The police sent Miss Burton to me. Inspector Podmore wrote to you that she was trying to find out the truth.'

Her face had gone quite blank. She nodded, and one hand went slowly over her forehead. 'I remember now. So you must be honest.' It sounded as though she found that fact surprising. Abruptly she held the door wide. She said, 'You'd better come in. I can't tell you anything you wouldn't already know, but you'll continue pestering us until we've spoken to you.'

She left them to close the door behind them. She went ahead, the sound of her neat black court shoes muffled on the softness of the grey carpeting. She went into a room to the left. She turned then to face them again, gestured behind her and said, 'My husband,' and then amended sharply, 'My ex-husband. We have divorced.'

'Why?' Shields gaze was taking in the tall figure outlined against the light from the big square windows, and seeing in him something of Sandra. The man was fair – as startlingly fair as the girl herself, but the lightness of his skin had the unhealthy tinge of a man who rarely saw the outdoors.

His eyes, surprisingly in a man so fair, were dark. They held anger as he nodded to Shields. He took longer over his inspection of Marion Burton. His gaze seemed to linger on her before he gave a short jerky bow.

It was the woman who said, real anger in her voice, 'That is none of your business!'

Shields dismissed the anger with a bland, 'It might be, if the reason was because of what happened four years ago. Did your marriage collapse because you knew that your daughter had lied, and one of you had insisted, against the other's wishes, on backing up those lies?'

Instinctively the woman had moved towards the man for protection against the words and the threat in them and, as instinctively as her own gesture, he had reached out and put his arm about her shoulders.

Glenn Kilby said quietly, 'You're quite wrong, and you're saying what a lot of other people said at the time of the divorce. You're quite wrong. Absolutely wrong.'

'Then, why?'

Kilby answered at last, after a long hesitation, 'Call it by the modern term of incompatibility. Tess resented my absorption in business, to the exclusion of the social life she wanted – that was one factor. There were others.'

'And have you' – Shield's gaze swung to the woman – 'gained the social life you wanted?' His gaze left her to travel the impersonal room, with its good but unexciting furnishings, its narrowness and its lack of anything approaching warmth. Whoever had decorated it had chosen without any real interest. Of that he was sure.

That his question had angered and upset her there was no doubt. She said, 'I haven't been well these last couple of years. I have had to lead a quiet life.' Dismissing that she asked, 'Mr Shields, what is the use of you coming here? Or staying here? If you want to ask such questions as this – about the divorce – what's the use? We've answered them so many, many times!'

He ignored the pleading in the word and her eyes.

He turned to Kilby and said, 'Mrs Kilby says you never employed anyone on a private investigation?'

Glenn Kilby shrugged. 'There was no use. The police told us that. Inspector Podmore was a good man – a first-class policeman and investigator. He found nothing.'

'Tell me – ' Shields was looking down at the wet hat that he was holding uneasily in his two hands. Neither of them had asked him to put it down, or had tried to take it from him or his coat, or Marion's either. It was an expression he knew, of their wish that he and Marion would go. He ignored it and simply went on looking in distaste at the wet black felt as he began again, 'Tell me, exactly what did Sandra say to you that night, when she first arrived home?'

Tess Kilby said sharply, 'Glenn didn't come in till later on. He'd been out all day. I was alone. Sandra said, when she came in, 'I've come home,' and when I asked why, she said, 'There was a man.' She added, 'He's dead.'

She said, with a quick glance at the other woman, 'I wrote you that. I sent you a long letter. There's nothing to add to what I wrote.'

Marion was going to speak, but Shields said, 'And then she told you the story she has kept to ever since?'

'She began to tell me,' she corrected. 'Glenn came home half way through and I called to him to come and then Sandra began again.'

'And when it was finished why didn't you both ring the police immediately? What made the two of you hold back from that if you believed Sandra was telling the truth? You couldn't have known that Peta was on her way home, with another version of the story to tell. Why didn't you ring the police?'

Glenn Kilby said, 'You're still asking questions we've answered over and over again. We didn't because the whole story sounded incredible. We couldn't believe, for a start, that Burton could really be dead. We turned on the news session. We learned that he truly was dead. We learned his name and we learned there was no apparent motive for his death.'

He added, 'Inspector Podmore told us that the other girl's family had heard that, too. Both of us waited. Perhaps it's hard to understand, but we were hoping, you see, that the true story need never come out. Do you think we looked forward to Sandra having to face police questioning, an appearance in court, with her word condemning another girl as a murderess? And she wasn't, you know – Burton's death was sheer terrible accident. He came between the two girls, and his stabbing wasn't meant to happen.

'We waited. We were wrong to do that, of course, but how we were expected to guess how it was going to turn out, I don't know, yet a lot of people threw doubt on us for just that point. We naturally thought that if the other girl was finally tied to Burton's death that she'd admit it. Do you think we even imagined that she would come up with the story she told and has kept to ever since?'

The same story, Shields was thinking. Always the same story, the same explanation, but told from another point of view.

He demanded, 'What happened to the road bible?'

Glenn Kilby said tiredly, 'What sense is there in asking us? If Sandra was innocent or guilty, we'd give the same answer. There never was such a thing.'

'Tell me what Sandra was like. I've read her statements and the words her teacher and the police wrote about her, and Peta's statements, but there's no statement of your own telling how Sandra appeared to your own eyes.'

The man looked at the woman. Their serious glances questioned and answered each other, then Glenn Kilby said, 'She was a lovable child. She was young for her age, and shy, a little awkward. New situations worried her. She liked to have someone's advice and help before acting. She worried a lot, I think, over the fact that she was not spectacular at anything – didn't stand out from the crowd. She was not particularly clever at schoolwork, and only average to poor in sport. Her dancing was quite fair and she enjoyed it, but that Christmas she had been depressed because she had been passed over for a part in the dancing school's Christmas show.'

He said helplessly, 'She was simply an average schoolgirl. Where's the help in that?'

Shields admitted, 'I don't know,' but he pressed, 'Was she untidy? Unpunctual? The type who put off things until tomorrow and – '

'Quite the opposite. She was very methodical, and she hated being late. That was Glenn's training.' Tess Kilby's voice was softer than it had been before. 'As an accountant he stressed the value of time and method to her. There was nothing in the least slovenly, off-hand, about her or her work. Her school reports were much the same, praising her for good preparation of projects and attention to detail and neatness.'

Her voice rose. She threw at him, 'When Sandra left here that summer holiday she was the same Sandra she had always been. She had a hundred plans for the year ahead. Do you really credit that she would risk destroying them all for the sake of a few wretched souvenirs?' She asked in astonishment, 'You're leaving?'

Jefferson Shields smiled at her. He said simply, 'Yes.'

He knew they were both standing on the landing, in that neat impersonal hallway, till the lift had gone from sight. He knew, too, that Marion was staring at him in real curiosity. She asked dryly, 'And just what was the purpose of that little exercise? Oh, yes, you'll say the same as you did before – that you wanted to see them. You haven't seen Peta's mother, or Mr Wincham.' The statement held question.

When he said nothing, only stood still in the foyer of the building, apparently waiting for her to go on, she said, 'Mr Wincham is at home. He took a week of his vacation leave. They know, of course, what I'm doing.' She added irritably, 'And we'll have to take a taxi, because it's a long way out.'

'They're still living at the same address?' He had agreed without argument to the taxi. She was sorry that she hadn't asked for one before as they settled back in the clammy warmth of it.

'Yes,' she agreed. 'Peta went away. I told you that, and Mr Wincham owns the house. He can be stubborn. He kept saying that they had nothing to be ashamed of, and that if they went away people might say they had. I don't know whether that's stubborn or brave or just being sensible, but they didn't move.'

'Sandra's schoolmistress said the Kilby family were comfortably off. That was four years ago. Has all this trouble made a difference there, would you say?'

'I doubt it. That apartment's expensive in spite of being small. Mine's even smaller,' she informed him candidly, 'and it costs the earth. Mrs Kilby doesn't work. She might possibly have an income of her own, but he didn't look down and out, did he? That suit was good. He has offices in a good building, too, and quite a few people working for him.'

She added, 'Mr Wincham hasn't much of a head for money. He makes a lot and most of it vanishes without him worrying about it. I'm afraid that's his attitude. The house needs painting again. It's not because they're poor or because he's slovenly or careless. It's just that he likes doing things round the place himself, but he never finds the time for half of them. He is' – she hesitated, then finished, 'rather a dear.'

Shields would have said disapproving. His build he had passed onto his son. They were very much alike. In Robert Wincham was the Ward of another thirty years hence. Only the eyes were different. Once they might have flashed green anger, like his son's. Now they were dulled and muted and hidden behind thick-lensed glasses.

He held the door – and it did need painting, as Shields noted – wide for them. He said, 'Hello, Marion,' and simply waited. Shields, watching him, thought that in his attitude was acceptance. He didn't want them there, but he was accepting it and not fighting it.

The woman echoed his attitude. She was plump and round-faced, with still dark hair and beautifully cared-for hands. She was proud of them. They lay flat in the lap of her well cut flame-coral dress, then the right one began gently stroking the back of the other. She kept on the slow, gentle, caressing movement while her glance questioned them.

Shields began, 'Can you remember what was the first thing Peta said to you when you returned home that night?'

'Oh, yes.' They answered together, then stopped, gave a brave little nod of apology to one another and then the woman went on alone.

'She was in her bedroom, with Ward. He had made her lie down. It's funny the mad way your mind works. I was frantic all that trip home wondering what had happened, yet when I ran into the bedroom the very first thing I thought of was that neither Ward nor Peta had remembered to pull back the spread, or remove her shoes!' She gave them a faint, wistful smile.

'Peta sat up when we ran in. She said quite clearly – she wasn't crying or anything like that, or even screaming the words out loud – she just sounded clear and straight about everything, and she said, 'She killed him, Mum, and what if she won't take the blame? What am I going to do?'

'Well, it sounded mad, and Ward broke in to say she had told him that someone was dead. You can imagine how we all felt, but Peta seemed quite clear about everything. She told us the lot from the time when she first met Sandra and she finished, 'I should have stayed and tried to help him, but he was dead – there was all that horrible blood.'

She shook her head. 'We made her see that if she'd stayed things might have been worse still, because that other girl might have tried to silence her with the knife. We should have rung the police, of course, and told them, but, well, we didn't. We waited, to see how it was going to turn out. I don't suppose it would have altered things if we had rung them there and then. The other girl would have been ready with her story. From what we learned afterwards she reached home hours before Peta got back here.'

She looked him full in the eyes as she said quietly, 'You know, of the two of them, I think it was the other one who suffered the most. That's a funny sort of thing for *me* to say, isn't it? But you see, Peta has a sort of self-sufficiency, a pride in herself. That's never been dented. She *knows* she's innocent, and she'd never been one to care much what other people think about her. We found out all we could about the other family. She was different from Peta. That school was only small, and she didn't seem to have friends outside the circle of it, so she lost all her friends and everything, and she wasn't self-sufficient like Peta. There was that divorce, too – we've often wondered about that. You know, when you look at them today, Peta's come out the best. I don't mean she's happy, because there'll always be the bitterness for her to remember, but she has work she likes, and it's the kind of thing she wanted to do and she's done quite well at it.

'This other girl – if things had been different, she wouldn't have the sort of life she has now. She would have gone through the usual social stages – dances and a proper coming out, and skiing parties and going on visits to country properties – a lot of her schoolfriends were boarders from big grazing properties. She would probably be engaged or married now and the boy would be well off. Perhaps would even have gone overseas with a group of her friends. There would have been university, too, if she'd gained enough credits. You see, she's missed all that.'

She added quite definitely, and there was a proud defiance in both expression and voice, 'Then, of course, she knows she's guilty. She can't have much respect for herself, can she?'

Robert Wincham spoke for the first time. He said dryly, 'There are people who can respect their own cleverness in fooling the world.'

Marion suddenly shivered. Suddenly she wished she hadn't come. She felt that in the dry comment there was a thrust of cruelty, of anger long buried and suddenly erupting, in a thrust perhaps at the woman who had turned a blank round face to meet his gaze.

She stood up, so violently that her fragile chair rocked back and she had to put out a hand to steady it. She saw the surprised faces turned towards her. She said, husky with embarrassment, 'I shouldn't have started all this. You're all of you right. You've all said everything you can and all this – it's so useless.' She rounded on Jefferson Shields, demanding, 'Isn't it?'

He said quite clearly, 'No.'

She didn't know what to say to that and after a little, when he simply ignored her, she sat down again, bewildered and embarrassed, because he was asking, 'Mr Wincham, you two must have talked together a great deal. Even if you felt you weren't close to Peta, you must have, in that year of being her stepfather, grown to know a lot about her. What was she like, in your eyes?'

He took his time to think over the question, then said finally, 'Her mother's told you. She had a self-reliance, an independence, a respect for herself. She wasn't vain,' he added quickly. 'Don't think that way, because it wouldn't be right. She just respected her abilities and her virtues and left it at that. So far as I could see she got along quite well with everyone, except myself, and don't go reading things into that. We both loved her mother and so we had something in common, but I think she felt the same as I did – that if we started the usual rough and tumble of families, the arguments and the sparring and give and take, that her mother would take sides in it, and the one seeming to be in the wrong would lose a bit of that love.

'I'm explaining things awkwardly.' His big face had reddened with embarrassment. 'But think that we pussy-footed round each other in a terrible plain of politeness and you'll have it. I didn't know how to get off the plain and up in the mountains and down in the valleys with her. It was different with Ward. They teased and argued and were up and down half a dozen times a day, only he wasn't around that much.

'I can sum up best by saying this. I've always loathed the whole business of hitch-hiking. I think it's wrong for a lot of reasons. I put my point of view to my wife that summer. She told me she didn't really approve either, but it was a growing trend, and Peta had proved over two summers that she could take care of herself and that the holidays were actually helping her to mature. She gave me chapter and verse and convinced me that was so. I decided that to try and impose my point of view would merely make Peta resent me.

'When Peta set out on that summer holiday she was as normal as ever, she had had no arguments or upsets with anyone, and she left home knowing she had the trust of us both. I can't – I just can't believe she would absurdly step out of character, because it would have forced her mother to side with me. The very thing Peta didn't want to see happening would definitely take place – her mother and I would become closer together and she would have been the other side of the fence, the outsider. Can you believe now that she started that souveniring business?'

17

'So neither of them lied. If you believe every word both sides say, you'd have to come to believe that neither girl lied, and that's impossible.'

Seated beside him again in another taxi, on the way back to the city, Marion said bitterly, 'I was a fool to start all this. It's easy to say to yourself when you start something, that you'll succeed in it and, when you watch the pile of papers growing, you gloat over them and think to yourself, It's all in there – all the truth of it and you think that because the stack of papers keeps growing that it *has* to be there. Then you find it isn't. I'm back where I started, and I'm so *tired*. Tired, do you understand? I want to stop it, because it's no good. One minute I think Peta lied, and the next I think, Oh no, it was Sandra, and I'm so tired that now I keep telling myself that it's all a mistake and neither of them lied, that neither of them stabbed Jack and stabbed him again and killed him and did all the rest of the things, either. I think neither of them lied.'

He said definitely, 'Oh, no. One lied. She was cunning and frightened and she lied very well, but she was helped.' There was a note she hadn't before heard in his voice. It sounded as though he was saying words he disliked speaking. 'She was helped and because she was helped she could never recover the lie or amend it or wash it away with the truth, because it would reveal her helper as a liar, too. In the end, you see, that burden was placed on her along with all the rest. She could never speak out, however much she might have wished to, without placing that other person in the position where, he or she, might go to gaol for what he had done for her.'

She told herself that she wasn't going to ask it. She knew a moment of sheer blinding terror, because she didn't want the name of the one who had lied, and she couldn't ask if he knew. She shrank back against the leather seat of the taxi, avoiding the glance of the grey eyes.

Shields said at last, 'That office of Mr Kilby's. Do you know where it is?'

'Yes,' The question came jerkily, raggedly, 'Are you going there? Why? You've already seen him and – '

'I want to see him without Mrs Kilby being present. Tell me,' the grey gaze sought hers and held it, 'if Ward Wincham was taken from your life, would it spoil your whole future? Can you imagine life without him and see it as an acceptable thing?'

She had gone quite white, but the probing gaze still held hers. She said at last, 'I – like him immensely. I – I suppose I've tried not to see into the future, but when I do it seems inevitable he'll always be around in mine.'

He said definitely, 'He doesn't love you. I told you he was a very ruthless man. Sandra Kilby was quite right when she spoke of it being incredible that you and Ward Wincham should have become friends. You yourself said something revealing about the situation. You said, 'We have things in common".

'But what things – purely, I think the fact that you were both connected with a mystery of four years standing. I doubt very much if the two of you would have come together otherwise. He is a hard, very mature man who spends his life roaming the world for business reasons, and, as you yourself have admitted, he spends his salary as he gets it – he had actually to borrow on his future salary when the crisis came and he wanted to hire an investigator. That is probably an attitude to money he has gained from his father. You, a rather gentle-natured woman would normally seek a husband among men who like an orderly business life. You would seek for a home, and security.

'You appear to me to be two different types, drawn together by what happened four years ago. I think that you have always keenly resented the fact that your brother's killer went scot-free. That would be a normal reaction, but there was nothing you could do about it. Private investigations are costly and when Jack Burton died you weren't very old and you had no parents alive to help you. You were also, as you told me, sick of the publicity.

'But it is four years later now. You are older, you have made a career for yourself and you have enough money to hire my services. Perhaps you have been thinking for some time of doing something about Jack's death. The difficulty would be to know where to start. You had met none of the people involved. If you had simply gone to one or the other family and said, "I'm going to investigate", both doors would have been closed to you.

'But knowing Ward Wincham gave you an entry to one family. Certainly you may like him very much and the fact that you have worked together on those reports for months shows that you get on well together, but Ward Wincham is a very ruthless man, as I warned you.

'I think he has used you. As you used him. He had no entry to the Kilby family. He had tried to see them and had been rebuffed. He couldn't force them to see him, but if Jack Burton's sister began the investigation – there was a different matter entirely. As Jack Burton's sister, as the entirely innocent character, and the bereaved one, and backed up by one family – would the other family have refused to co-operate? Of course not. They would fear you would see only one side of the story and be biased by it. They'd be eager to give their own side.

'I told you he is used to weighing up facts quickly and making decisions. He saw the possibilities in you and he has used you. I think you were correct in saying he is devoted to his father. He has spoken himself in his statement of how his father and stepmother have drawn apart, while remaining married. For a young man who was devoted to his father and had hoped him to find happiness in a second marriage, that must have been very bitter. He has probably watched them over the years grown further and further away from each other.

'Then he met you, and he sees in you a chance of entry to the Kilby family. He might like you. He possibly respects you and is certainly grateful to you for all your work.' He added simply, 'You would be extremely foolish if you delude yourself of anything more.'

She demanded, 'Why tell me this now? Why – '

'Because I am going to prove, quite definitely, that one girl lied and, when I have proved it, unless you have faced up to the facts I've just pointed out to you, you are going to be gravely hurt.'

18

The office spoke quite definitely of money and money carefully applied to the best advantage. It was comfortable and
well furnished and the wide windows overlooked the gardens
of the city.

Seated behind the black-beam wood desk, Glenn Kilby
seemed a bigger man that the slight figure outlines against the
window of his ex-wife's apartment.

His voice was curter, too. It hinted at time passing, at
appointments put off and work waiting. He suggested, 'I can
hardly help you further.'

'I think so,' Shields told him. 'One thing struck me, Mr
Kilby. Although four years have passed since that other
January, no private investigation has ever taken place, but
questioning, I have come on reasons.

'Marion Burton,' he gave a little nod to the silent woman
on the other side of the office, 'was only nineteen herself. She
was shocked and bereaved, and she had no family left to help
and support her, and very little money. She wished, also, only
to hide from the publicity and the memory of what had happened to her brother.

'Robert Wincham had no savings. Neither did his wife.
Ward Wincham, however, borrowed on his future salary and
tried to find an investigator. He was rebuffed. One told him
the case was impossible of solution if the police work had
failed to turn up one. The other suggested it could be solved –

at a price, because faked evidence could be brought to prove that Sandra had lied.'

The fair head jerked up and Kilby's mouth tightened.

'I have already explained to Miss Burton that in my opinion Ward Wincham was as much in the dark as the police. If he had been even fairly certain that his stepsister was innocent, he would have accepted in the hope that your daughter would crack under the pressure of that new onslaught and tell the truth. He didn't take that risk. Either he knew that she had lied, or he couldn't be sure she had told the truth. That the latter was right I am sure. If he had known for a certainty that Peta was the one who had lied four years ago, he would never have sought out Marion Burton and encouraged her to re-open the investigation. If he was sure, from the beginning, that Peta had lied, he would never have approached any investigator at all in the first place. He would have wanted the enquiry to stop.

'Now we come to you and your wife, Mr Kilby. You were comfortably off. Certainly there was no shortage of ready cash that anyone knew about. Yet you say yourself you made no attempt, and have never made any since, to have the matter re-opened.'

'I told you.' The fair head lifted and the eyes met the other man's glance and held it. 'I told you the reason. I was told by the inspector that it would be useless.'

'How could you be sure, without trying? You were a man facing up to his daughter's possible ruin and heartbreak. It's nowhere near reasonable, Mr Kilby, that you wouldn't have taken some chance of another opinion. Ward Wincham tried. He was rebuffed of course, but why didn't you *try*, Mr Kilby?'

'Podmore told me I'd be rebuffed. He said that any honest firm would tell me I was wasting time and money and the other type would simply waste both.'

'And you accepted that? Or was it because you were afraid that new evidence *might* turn up, if a new investigator looked at the case?'

To Marion it seemed that the other man was quite unperturbed by the challenge. He said, almost lightly, 'You're groping in the dark, Mr Shields. You can't tell how another man would react, unless you've faced such a situation, been in the thick and bitterness of it, yourself. I had faith in Podmore. Leave it at that. Is that all?'

'No. When I read through the reports that Miss Burton had gathered, I was struck by one thing – the mention of a road bible, the reason Peta gave for the name of Saint Kilby that she gave to your daughter.

'I was struck first by its air of complete *truth*. It was an utterly plausible, utterly believable story, and it fitted quite well with what you yourself said of Sandra's character – that she was methodical, and went about projects with great care and effort. It seemed utterly believable that a girl of Sandra's type should keep a notebook of hints about hitch-hiking for future reference and future projects.

'I think that was the point that Inspector Podmore saw for himself. It was plausible from what Sandra herself claimed. Her story held many examples of advice from her companion. Her aim, naturally, was to show how completely dependent she was, in her ignorance, on Peta Squire – to give an adequate reason why their association continued. In this she succeeded. We gain the impression of an ignorant girl needing help and clinging to the only helper who came forward, but it seems to me that she remembered those pieces of advice so well that she had taken careful note of them before her return home, probably in a notebook. A road bible, as Peta claims.

'It is not, either, the type of story that a girl would think up by herself. If it was a lie, an excuse to cover that nickname, it had an adult ring to it.'

'Her parents – ' Glenn Kilby began, but the other man brushed the interruption aside.

'Listen to the evidence. Peta Squire came home. In the presence of three people she recited the story that she was later to tell the police. If she was lying, her whole story would have dwelt on two important points – she was *not* the one who stole things, and she was *not* the one who stabbed and killed Jack Burton. The fact that she had called the other girl "Saint Kilby" might not have been touched on. If she had remembered about it then, or if she was asked about it later and needed an excuse other than the truth, why not say the obvious? Why not say simply, "Her name was S.T. Kilby. She told me the second name – the name of a saint. I called her Saint Kilby."'

'There was an obvious reason right at hand. Even the police had thought of it. But, no, she ignores it and starts an involved story of a notebook that Sandra called her "road bible".'

Glenn Kilby said, 'There's no knowing what anyone would do, trying to squirm out of trouble. She might completely have forgotten Sandra's second name.

'It's possible, but to me that story of the road bible had a ring of truth, so now we look at Sandra's version. She objected to Peta's souveniring and she objected strongly. She stood up for her own views there – so she claimed – and for it was immediately dubbed "Saint". That wasn't in jest. Thrown at her, in that context, it was a taunt, a jeer at her own stated convictions. What girl wouldn't have struck back instantly, objecting to the taunt, the jeer and the name? Yet what happened? If Sandra's version is true, she did nothing at all, and for the rest of their trip she meekly accepted the taunt of "Saint" thrown at her whenever her companion chose.

'That has a ring of complete untruth.'

In the quiet of the room, the murmur of the air conditioner seemed to grow louder. Jefferson Shields's voice drowned it again as he went on, 'Sandra would be well prepared with her version, because one of the first things her parents would have said, when her story was told, would have been, "But we thought the fair girl's name was Saint-something!"'

'You'd read the press story, and heard the television and radio call for the girls. Mrs Kilby's statement says so. If Sandra had not remembered that point, she would have been swiftly reminded. She would have been ready with her reason for the name by the time police reached her.

'When I had realised that, I went through all those statements again, looking for something else that said to me, "Here is untruth" or, "Here is something with the ring of truth." For all my reading I gained absolutely nothing. Each story could have been true, right to the last tragedy when Jack Burton died, when each girl said the same thing, that the knife went into the man's body, that he clutched his chest, and that the bloodied knife was held aloft again, as the girl fled.

'It was then I realised that neither claimed to have seen that second blow struck. I suddenly wondered, What if it was never struck at all? But that was absurd. The medical evidence said he was struck twice. So had Marion Burton. That fact was not in doubt, so a second blow was struck.

'Go back over the evidence, as I did. Try to visualise that scene. There was one girl, a shocked witness, who fled. There was another, hysterical in rage, who had stabbed a man who had rushed between the two girls. She still holds the knife – that sounds as though that first wound was not particularly deep. She swings back that knife – bloodied, and sees what Peta described as "all that horrible blood" and she sees the man clutching at his chest. Far from striking at him again – remember, she had no real quarrel with him – he had simply stepped between her and the other girl. I think she would have realised what she had done and dropped the knife, never striking another blow at all.

'The more I thought about it, the more that idea seemed feasible, yet the plain fact remained: he was struck twice and neither girl had ever questioned the fact that two blows were struck.

'That seemed to place the final doubt on my idea. If the girl with the knife had suddenly seen clearly and realised what she had done, and dropped the knife without striking a second blow, wouldn't she have said so? In that statement there was a way to clear herself. Of course, subsequent investigations might never have turned up the person responsible, but how could she know that would happen? She would have hoped and expected that she would be cleared, and she would have spoken out.

'She must have struck two blows. I visualised that scene as I had done before. I tried to imagine a girl so enraged, and so lost in that rage, that she was unable to realise what she had just done.

'I couldn't. It seemed almost a certainty to me that she had never realised in that first thrust that she had stabbed with the knife at all.

'I kept thinking about it. I wondered suddenly if, while that first blow had been an accident, the second had not – that it had been struck deliberately – to silence. I wondered, What if that girl had been so ruthless that she had struck viciously and deliberately to silence Jack Burton, so that he could never speak out and say what she had done?

'It seemed incredible, and yet – I found it equally incredible that she should have been in such a blind rage that that terrible sight of the blood and the wounded man hadn't brought her to her senses before she struck the second blow.

'I went over it again. I tried to imagine that someone else could have struck that second blow. That was equally incredible. Jack Burton had no enemies. Even if there had been one, who could believe in the coincidence that one should appear at that moment?

'Inspector Podmore had spoken of queer types who go to a scene in the news and hover about it. He had, at first, wondered if some mentally deranged person hadn't come on Jack Burton and stabbed him. The theory was far-fetched and, more so, if you tried to visualise anyone coming on that shocking scene – remember "all that horrible blood" – and picking up the knife and stabbing Burton once more, simply because of mental derangement.

'The idea was ridiculous, and that left the position as it had been in the beginning. One of those girls had stabbed twice. What I couldn't rid myself of was the idea that the second blow must have been done deliberately – to silence.

'I tried to think which of them could have been so coldly ruthless. It was impossible, and then suddenly I thought of someone who might be so coldly ruthless, who could have been the striker of that second blow, to silence. There was only one type of person, to my mind, in all concerned, who could have acted in that way, someone so close to one of those girls that he or she struck in panic, to silence Burton and protect the girl.

'There in front of me was a reason why the girl had never said, "I struck only one blow." All along she had struck only once, but she has known, just as definitely, who struck the second time. Just as the blow was struck to protect her, she was forced to protect in her turn and to remain silent.

'Mr Kilby, human nature is inclined to think in clichés about a disaster. Many statements referred to this one as a landslide, and that was true. I have seen a landslide myself in New Zealand. It began with a pebble, and the pebble dislodged stones, and the stones dislodged boulders till there was one appalling crash that crushed a bridge. Everyone spoke of the way the landslide had finished in destroying that bridge, just as everyone spoke of Jack Burton's death as the final tragedy.

'But sometimes a landslide hides another tragedy. That one in New Zealand did. It wasn't until a fortnight afterwards that a man – a bushwalker – was found to be missing. All that time his body had been under that landslide. There had been a final disaster, hidden from everyone.

'The more I went over those statements, and facts, the more sure I became that here there had been a hidden tragedy, too. Everyone had seen the obvious – the fact that a girl had stabbed a man. They hadn't looked beyond and beneath that one fact.

'I did, and I knew, Mr Kilby, that I could be right.'

Glenn Kilby sat very still. His hands were clasped loosely in front of him. He said nothing at all.

Jefferson Shields went on gently, 'Look at the evidence again. On that Sunday it was normal in the Wincham home. Ward had a broken ankle and was on crutches. Mr and Mr Wincham spent an ordinary day and in the evening they went to visit friends.

'No one had said what Mrs Kilby was doing, but you Mr Kilby were, in her own words, "out all day and came home after Sandra".

'Think back to Saturday evening. Both radio and television reported the tragedy in Asherton where a child and a man had been poisoned and the man had crashed his car. This was followed by an appeal for two girls to come forward. That was followed by an interview described as appalling.

'In the Wincham house they probably saw and heard it all, and what of it? They knew two girls were wanted for taking that box. One girl's name was Winchely. That night they learned her name was Peta. But what was Peta Winchely to Peta Squire? Nothing at all, and I have noted one important point – although the police knew the girl had a large mole on her left hand that fact was omitted from the police appeal on Saturday evening.

'Another point – I am certain they could have had no knowledge of that clown costume. Peta says herself that she made it in secret. She wouldn't have been likely to show it to Ward. Ward would have teased and mocked her. She wouldn't have shown it to Mr Wincham. He was against her hitch-hiking. He might have objected to the costume. For the same reason she wouldn't have told her mother, for fear her mother would inform Mr Wincham.

'So nowhere was there a clue to tell the Wincham family that Peta was in serious trouble. For them that Saturday evening and the Sunday were normal. There was nothing that could have taken any of them to Asherton.

'But look at Sandra's character. Something stands out. You indulged her, and her mother was the one to say no. Her mother said no to hitch-hiking, but you were indulgent. You had actually been on her side to allow her to have that holiday alone. You wanted her to learn to stand on her own feet. Sandra, however, was not one to do things on her own initiative – she liked advice and backing. I think she wanted you on her side, too. I think it very likely she told you she intended to hitch-hike if she found a suitable friend and that she pleaded that it would help to untie her mother's apron strings.

'Did you agree, so that she went off happily? She would have reasoned that if her mother found out, you would have known, so the blame would rest on you.

'There was another thing that had struck me from the beginning. Why had Sandra, shy, afraid of new experiences, chosen to go on a holiday alone? Surely through those seven weeks of the long summer vacation one of her school friends could have found time to go with her? Yet she went alone. Doesn't it seem likely that she was about to do something that might get back to her mother's ears?

'Were you worried, Mr Kilby, when you read that first report of a girl with long fair hair? Did you suddenly remember that Sandra's initials on her pack were S.T. Kilby and that they might have been mistaken for St-something?

'You could have done nothing – then. You didn't know where she was but, on Saturday night, you saw and heard the television reports and now, suddenly, you hear and see a man in such a raging temper speaking of a "prissy little miss with mock innocent grey eyes".

'Did you suddenly see Sandra standing there in front of you? Perhaps you couldn't bring yourself to believe it. Or had she told you of the souveniring? If she had, you would have said no, I am certain, but still – here was a prissy little miss with butter on her tongue and mock innocent grey eyes, with a long fair plait and a name that might be St-something.

'I think, Mr Kilby, you had to find out. You left home and drove to Asherton through the night, even if you had no real way of finding Sandra. You just had to know if she could possibly be the wanted girl. You were probably hoping that the girl would have been cornered by the time you reached Asherton and that it wouldn't be Sandra.

'You arrived, and what then? You were faced with doing nothing. Nobody could tell you anything. You were at a loose end. Did you go then to Asherton Park to stare at the pond where the box was found?

'However it happened, it is quite feasible that you went to the park and stumbled on Sandra, either in the act of running away, of committing the stabbing, or that you stumbled on Jack Burton and he told you the fair girl had stabbed him.

'Whatever it was, the knife was there. Did you kill him, Mr Kilby, to save Sandra from prison? Only to realise too late that you had condemned yourself and Sandra, too, to eternal lies?

'You have told how you sat back and prayed that the story need never come out. It appeared in the beginning that Burton's death might be classified as a mystery. You hoped it would be, for ever. Even if you had the courage, and the ruthlessness, to go to the police in the beginning, and to clear Sandra completely by stating you had been in the park and had seen, not Sandra, but Peta, commit the stabbing, what excuse could you have given for being in the park in the first place?

'None, and you must have known it. To admit the true reason for your going was to make nonsense of Sandra's story and yours. To claim that a telegram had come from her could be disproved easily. The same with a trunkline call.

'After Burton's death, you must have lost her in Asherton. Perhaps you wasted a great deal of time trying to find her, but you didn't. You had to drive home alone. You arrived after she had.'

Glenn Kilby lifted his hands. He sat looking at them, as though remembering what they had once done. He let them fall. He said slowly, 'I kept expecting someone to guess. They were blinded, of course. It's the way you say it. Everyone spoke of it finishing with Burton's stabbing by one of the girls. That was so horrible, no one ever looked any further.

'I saw the girls. All you've said is quite true. You're very clever.' There was a grave acknowledgment in his voice. 'I knew about the hitch-hiking, and Sandra told me of that stupid dare. I wouldn't agree to that, of course. I told her not to play the fool, but I agreed she could hitch-hike. If it worked out well, it would be a signpost for future holidays.

'And you're right about that night. With that dreadful, convulsed, *hating* face staring at me from the screen, I saw Sandra – the prissy little miss with the mock innocent eyes. I was terrified. I jumped into the car with only one idea – to get to her – but once I was in Asherton I didn't know what to do.'

'I went to the pond. I don't know why. There were a lot of people around and I turned away. Then I saw the girls. They were together, walking across the park, hurrying. I almost called to her then, but I was afraid of other people hearing and seeing them too.

'I saw them reading the paper, and then Sandra became hysterical. I didn't know whether to interfere or not. I'd been standing out of sight, watching and listening. I'd been afraid of stepping into sight for fear Sandra would go to pieces at the sight of me and I'd have difficulty in quietening her, and people would be drawn to the scene.

'All of a sudden the girls started quarrelling. When I saw that knife it was so frankly unbelievable that I just stood staring. Where Burton was I don't know. He came rushing into sight and everything was so fast it was over before I could move. Both girls were running, and Burton was doubled up on the grass. I ran to him, first, to see how badly he was hurt. He was alive and furiously angry. He yelled at me, "That damned little witch! She deserved ten years for this! Get the police!"

'Yes, he asked for the police, not a doctor. I don't know how badly he was hurt, but obviously he wasn't too worried.

It was what he said though – about Sandra getting ten years, and then demanding the police – I went crazy. I must have. I'd been driving all night, and I was exhausted and frantic with worrying. It was over before I realised I'd even picked up the knife. Perhaps Sandra and I are much of a type. We panic at danger and disaster.

'I did try finding her in Asherton. I tried for hours, and then I knew it was hopeless, so I drove home.' He stopped. He seemed to be reflecting, and Shields made no attempt to interfere.

Finally Kilby said, 'Sandra has known. All this time she's known. You're right there, too. She's had that added bitterness and burden. I struck to protect her and then – you see, at first there wasn't much news. Just an account of a man stabbed to death. It didn't say how many times he'd been stabbed. Then at the inquest there was the medical evidence. None of us appeared at it. We had doctors to say that Sandra was too ill to attend, but the evidence was in the paper.

'I remember the moment when she lifted her eyes and said in a shocked voice, "But they're wrong. It's quite wrong. I only hit him once! Just once! *Only* once. When I saw him and all that blood I dropped the knife and I ran away. I thought he was dead then, but I didn't stab him twice." And then she looked at us in bewilderment and she said, "Someone else must have stabbed him." I remember the excitement in her face and the way she wanted to tell the police then.

'Perhaps my face gave me away to Tess. She knew I'd been away all that night and the Sunday. I'd given her the excuse of business. That was always enough to quieten her. She detested any talk of it. But that day she drew me aside. She knew. She tackled me, and I had to tell her because we had to quieten Sandra.

'You see' – his voice was bitter – 'it was too late. If I'd gone to the police then and told the truth, they'd have arrested me and put me on trial; there would always have been half the country to say that I'd taken the blame for my daughter, and to point the finger of hate at her. And if she was tried? Don't you see how impossible it was to speak out? It was too late. I'd trapped the lot of us in those lies.

'Sandra knew I'd done it for her sake. She has never said one word of reproach, but I thought it better to go away. Tess made no objections. So we divorced.'

He added simply, 'It's very lonely, living a lie.'

19

Marion said, and her voice shook with indignation, 'You let me think it was Peta. You told me not to go on thinking about Ward. You let me think it was Peta and, because of that, because I'd been the one who'd pried into the case, I'd never be welcome in the Wincham family. You let me think – '

'Did I say any of that? I told you to forget Ward Wincham and I warned you that he had used you.' He drew her into the shelter of a neighbouring shop doorway, out of the slanting downpour. 'I have seen him once. One thing was evident even so. He is in love with Peta. He's no blood relation. Why shouldn't he be? Perhaps it was pity and compassion that drew them together in the beginning, but it is love now. He is devoted to her. She loves him, too, I think, but she has trained herself never to show any emotion any more. As Sandra said – they are both conditioned and hardened never to show anything. She's been afraid to show anything, or speak out. Perhaps she feels that Mr Wincham will hardly want her for his son, hardly accept grandchildren through her.

He asked, 'Where are we going?'

'I don't know.' She was shaken and bewildered and yet a load seemed to have gone from her shoulders. It wasn't just that she knew who had lied. It was something else. She wanted to face that, and face it alone.

She asked, 'Why did you leave Mr Kilby alone? He might run away. He might – '

'He finished running a long time ago. I think he has been waiting, for all that time, for someone to stumble on the truth. Almost certainly he has rung his wife and told her. He has probably by now rung the police and asked them to come.

'My own phone call, just now, was to Peta.'

She turned, and lifted her gaze. She asked huskily. 'What did she say?'

'She asked me to wait. To come to her in an hour. To tell her then all about it. She said to me, "I must have time to get used to it. I must have time to – thaw, before I can listen and accept it." She told me I wouldn't understand, but I do.' He nodded soberly. 'She has had all emotion in deep storage. You could say that and be right. I understand very well.'

She thought, You understand too much, and she stood there watching him till he was a blur in the grey slanting rain, a short, nonentity of a man in a crumpled plastic raincoat and wet black velvet felt hat. Then she began to walk herself, long strides that took her faster and faster, as though, she were trying to run from all that happened.

———

Patricia Carlon was born in Wagga Wagga in 1927. She was educated at various schools in New South Wales before settling in Sydney. She continues to write, is a prize-winning cook, a keen gardener and lives surrounded by her cats.

She has written everything from articles, short stories and serials to short and long novels. Her work has been published in Australia and England under various names in daily papers, magazines and on radio. Much of her pseudonymous writing has been romantic fiction, under the name Barbara Christie, for example. Her most substantial work, however, encompasses crime and thriller novels, of which she has published at least fourteen. These were first published between 1961 and 1970 in England, mostly by Hodder and Stoughton in the King Crime series. Many have also been published in other European countries and her work has been translated into seven languages.

She was awarded Commonwealth Literary Fellowships in 1970 and 1973.

The Souvenir was chosen by Foyles as its Thriller Book Club choice in 1971, and it is one of the author's favourites. It is a first-rate modern crime novel, modern in the sense that it combines the elements of detection and suspense and has echoes of other women crime writers, other fictional detectives. We are reminded of Anthony Gilbert (Lucy Beatrice Malleson) and Patricia Wentworth, although it is in the character of the improbably named Jefferson Shields that engages memory most firmly. Sherlock Holmes and Nero Wolfe come to mind, although neither are so purely ratiocinative as Shields - who, also, has no committed helper and who does all all his own leg-work. While Marion, in *The Souvenir*, acts as his foil to some extent in the climactic series of interviews, Shields presents his solutions to puzzles by reading official reports, witnesses' statements, and protagonists' versions of events. These, he passes through the porous membranes of human anxieties and fears, and eventually finds the motive which provides the sequence of emotions which lead to the puzzle's solution.

Shields is Carlon's triumph in this book. After the opening chapter (echoes of Sam Spade and the Continental Op) he virtually disappears from the narrative until chapter fifteen (of nineteen) yet when he reappears at that late stage the reader has been waiting for him all along to take charge.

For such expectation, and grateful relief, we have to thank Carlon's careful, dense plotting. It is a narrative based entirely on the 'ordinary', a condition made much of by Inspector Podmore in his written statement to Marion Benton (in a chapter which contains an important clue gently laid down by Carlon), a crime of ordinary, everyday people. The ordinariness is almost suffocating in its details, from the descriptions of the tedious business of hitch-hiking and of staying in hostels; the mean suspicions of car drivers. café owners, shopkeepers; the mounting, tantalising details of Peta's and Sandra's characters and lives. This is all part of Patricia Carlton's method, the layers of facts and concrete details relieved by small ironic counterpoints - the stress on the bushes of Crepe Myrtle when the two girls rest in Asherton Park; Sandra as St. Teresa. Carlton's firm commonsensical opinions about contemporary cultural issues, such as the encouragement of young women in their own freedoms are deftly worked into the narrative, all underpinned by a clearly focused tolerance. But, after the exhaustive, inconclusive layering of evidence and speculation, Shields is the only one to whom we, as readers, can turn.

The brilliantly described opening scene craftily creates what the man is not - ordinary. In so doing, Carlton keeps the character at bay as it were, saving him for the denouement. This grey 'nonentity' solves human and criminal puzzles through the power of his mind and the ruthlessness of his perceptions, unfettered by much ordinary human sympathy we might add - the way he disabuses poor Marion of her long-held romantic notions for Ward Wincham border on the arrogantly cruel. Yet, with all his faults - unattractive, almost inert, 'crow-like', dangerous (Marion judges, 'you understand too much'), this crumpled genius deserves to be recognised among the memorable omniscient private detectives of literature. His brief life in fiction is our loss.

PETER MOSS AND MICHAEL J. TOLLEY

———

SOHO CRIME

Other Titles in this Series

JANWILLEM VAN DE WETERING

Outsider in Amsterdam
Tumbleweed
The Corpse on the Dike
Death of a Hawker
The Japanese Corpse
The Maine Massacre
The Blond Baboon
Just a Corpse at Twilight

SEICHO MATSUMOTO

Inspector Imanishi Investigates

MARTIN LIMÓN

Jade Lady Burning

JIM CIRNI

The Kiss Off
The Come On
The Big Squeeze

TIMOTHY WATTS

Cons
Money Lovers

CHARLOTTE JAY

Beat Not the Bones